The Trouble With Angels

BY

JORDYN MERYL

Other Books
By
Jordyn Meryl

When Dreams Change

Home Before Dark

Summer of 2012

Echoes of the Midnight Star

Book One

Katrina-Star Goddess

Book Two

Zalie-Star Child

Book Three

Zale-Star Warrior

The Trouble With Angels

BY

JORDYN MERYL

jm dragonfly L.L.C.
Des Moines, IA

The Trouble With Angels
by Jordyn Meryl

Published by jm dragonfly, L.L.C.
Des Moines, IA
Copyright © May 2012
By Jordyn Meryl

First Printing: May 2012
ISBN-13: 978-1477432365
ISBN-10: 1477432361
Printed in the United States of America
Cover Design-EJR Digital Art-www.ejrdigitalart.com
Author photograph-Trish Toma-Lark

To my Guardian
Angels.
You guide me,
protect me and
enriched my life.
I love you
jm

A strong woman
can always
capture love in
the right pair of
shoes.
...Jordyn Meryl

CHAPTER ONE

"What the fuck? Seriously?"

"Oh damn, I am so sorry." The deep male voice came from the large, sturdy body that slammed into Paige Therriault. Her long auburn hair tumbled to her shoulders as her trendy women's newsboy cap fell off her head.

Oh, hell no! This is Monday morning. Not happening.

Spilling her fresh, white chocolate latte on her black coat, the man's arms steadied her as she started to fall back. Catching her balance, the plastic cup slipped out of her wet hand, landing on the sidewalk, splashing the black expensive Italian leather shoes of her assailant.

Shaking the remainder of the coffee from her now empty hands, she huffed and looked up at the man's face. Stopped cold by the most beautiful eyes, shiny and dark as wet slate, she had ever saw. Her words frozen in her throat.

"Are you all right?" His voice, polished and soothing was full of concern.

Numb, all she could do was nod. The handsome man holding her was taking her breath away. Some kind of chemistry she had never felt before was flowing between them.

Taking a step back out of his grip. "I'm...fine." Brushing away the coffee beading up on her water-repellent trench coat, feeling her face get red, she was wanting to get away from this person, this..

God he's good-looking.

...man blocking her path to work. But he wasn't budging. He took a linen handkerchief from his pocket and was dabbing at the remaining coffee on the front of her coat. Even though his touch was light and barely felt through the heavy material, just the gentleness was bringing her a sweet reaction to him.

Again she stepped back and hit a lamp pole with her head.

Damn that hurt.

Tears sprang to her eyes, again the man was touching her. Holding her up with his strong arms.

His eyes reflected his concern. "Watch it. Here let me get you to where you are going."

There was a long awkward pause between them.

She lost herself in his eyes again, so dark, so deep, so...

His voice cut through her thoughts. "Where are you going?"

Shaking her hurting head, breaking away from his hold, she looked around. Then up at the building they were standing in front of.

"Here, I work here."

Get it together, girl.

Hiking her messenger bag/brief case back on her shoulder, she straightened her back. The man picked up her cap from the sidewalk.

I just bought this damn hat.

Snatching it from his hand, she squared her shoulders as if she was totally back in control. "Thank you for your help, Mr. ...?"

"Winston. Mark Winston. I work here too. I'll go in with you. Make sure you make it okay."

Paige stopped short. "Winston? Of Winston, Bradley and Smart Ad Agency?"

His smile was dazzling. "Yes, that would be me. Well kind of. I'm Tom's youngest son. You know of us?"

"Yes, I work for you." Her smile as well as her spirit was weak. "I'm your Art Director. Paige Therriault." She heard the younger son of the boss was joining 'the team'. The prodigal son returning home type of thing.

Optimistically he took her arm. "Well good, I'll walk you up. You can show me around."

Sure thing. What a great way to make an impression.

***

"Way to go slick. You almost gave her first degree burns." The first angel said to the second, sitting together on the newsstand watching Mark and Paige go inside.

"Sorry, but I needed them to meet before they met at work."

"And why is that?" The first angel was a beautiful, dark-skinned male that had not really wanted this assignment in the first place.   Let alone with the angel of Never-Ending Love.

"Meeting at work inhibits the spirit. Bumping into each other is fate, kismet."

Rolling his eyes the second male angel was fair-skinned, handsome and adorable.

"Well they met. What do we do now?"

The second angel's wings fluttered. "We go watch what happens." Following cute and adorable, the dark angel asked. "You weren't by any chance on the Titanic, were you?"

***

Standing in front of the elevators waiting for the doors to open, Paige tried not to touch Mark's shoulder. With him still holding her arm, she was trying to put as much space between them as she could so he would let go. But the morning rush of workers was knocking them together. It wasn't that she disliked Mark Winston. Since he just appeared on the scene, so to speak. And only good things were ever said about him.

The doors opened and a horde of

people ushered them into the small square space. Now she was plastered up against him, chest to chest. His cologne, while a refreshing musk scent, was making her feel an attraction to this handsome, kind man.

Since there was no other place to look, she took in the features of his face. The eyes captured her first, but his skin was a light tan with just a crinkle around his eyes that said he smiled a lot. He was smiling now, down at her. His lips were quite close and quite appealing. She gave him a weak grin.

His sun-tipped hair with an expensive cut and style. Clean shaven, he didn't support the rough, unkempt look of so many men these days. Paige liked the sharp, smooth face appearance. The only time she enjoyed seeing a man with facial hair was when she woke up next to him in the morning.

Stop it!

One of his hands was on her waist, steadying her as the occupants joshed them closer to each other. His breath was warm on her neck. There were ten floors to go. As the elevator stopped and released some of the people, room opened for her to move around. She turned her back to him and moved closer to the wall.

Her hands were sticky from the spilled coffee. She felt ruffled and out of whack. As the bell rang for the tenth floor, the doors opened and there was Mr. Bradley, Mr. Smart and the elder Mr. Winston.

"Mark, you made it." Tom Winston's pride for his son radiated on his face.

Mark stepped around her, started to say something to her, but Paige darted behind him and made a hasty escape to her office. She was greeted at the doorway by her assistant, Amy. Cute, young and always perky, but today Paige wasn't quite ready for the blonde, curly haired, 'loving life' Amy.

"What in the world happened to you?" Amy helped Paige remove the soiled coat. Amy was Paige's right hand and dearest friend.

When Paige arrived the first day at the agency, Amy cut right to the chase. Paige was the boss. Amy was there to see that Paige's guidelines were followed. They were to work together. Over the last two years Amy became Paige's confidant and major supporter.

Paige worked her arms out of the sleeves. "Don't ask. Will you send this to the cleaner's downstairs?"

Holding the collar, coffee still dripping off, Amy exchanged the coat for phone messages. "Sure thing. Hey have you seen Mark Winston yet? I hear he is some kind of gorgeous."

"Yeah, I have." Paige shuffled the papers in her hand.

Amy's voice went an octave higher. "You have? Where? When?"

Paige's answer was to slam her office door on the questions. Going to her desk she plopped down in the huge desk chair and swung around to look out the window at the dull gray day.

"Paige, your Mom is on line one. Are you okay?" Amy's voice filtered through the intercom.

Paige turned back around to her desk. "Yes, I'm okay Amy. Just a rough start to the morning. I'm better now, thank you."

Slipping the Bluetooth over her ear, Paige pressed it on. "Mom?"

"Pagie, listen how would you like to spend Christmas in the sun, surf and sand?" Her voice was brimming with excitement.

"Hum, hadn't thought of it." Paige didn't know if the idea excited her or not. "Why?"

"Think Mexico. Beautiful resort. Everything provided. What'd ya' say?"

Since Paige's parents divorced, her mother stopped doing traditional holidays. Last Christmas was spent on a cruise ship touring Alaska. At least this year they were going someplace warmer.

"Sure. Look into it. We still on for dinner tomorrow night?" Paige flipped on her computer.

"Of course. Diego's. How fitting. Mexican food and I'll bring all the stuff about our trip. Bye' Hon, Love ya'."

"Bye, love you too." Paige clicked off the connection.

As she waited for her computer to boot-up, Amy brought in a cup from Paige's favorite coffee shop. Amy lifted one eyebrow as she sat it on the desk.

Paige eyed the cup, raised her eyes to Amy.

Amy answered her unspoken question. "Mr. Winston." A mischievous smile lit up her face. "Mr. Mark Winston." With a heavy accent on Mark.

The cup of coffee made Paige get a nervous kick in her stomach. She stared at it.

It was a kind gesture, but why? The man is the shinning heir to the company. Why would he care if an employee dropped a cup of coffee? Especially since it was on his shoes.

Amy left slowly, backing out of the office, closing the door with a soft click.

"Amy." Paige shouted after her.

The door opened just a crack. "Yes?"

Paige cocked her head to one side. "How did Mr. Winston know what kind of coffee I drank?"

Amy crinkled her eyes. "I told him?"

"He asked?" Paige was thinking of what his motives might be.

Amy opened the door a little

more. "Yes, when he asked where your coat was. Problem boss?"

Paige waved Amy out. "No, just figured the man would have more to do than get coffee and ask about my dry cleaning."

Amy's chuckle didn't escape Paige's ears. After the door was closed Paige took the coffee cup in her hands. All the expectations of this one coffee cup clouded her mind. She would have to thank him. In person? E-mail? Cute little card? Get real. A professional thank you card? More protocol.

Taking a sip of the sweet warm liquid, it did taste good. And since she hardly got a drink of hers this morning, this was a welcome treat.

Okay I will figure it out later. Right now I am going to enjoy my first real cup of coffee. ***

The two angels sat on the bookcase watching Paige.

Cute and adorable licked his finger and made a sparkling silver blue mark in the air. "Score one for the big guy." The mark disappeared.

Dark and grumpy hissed. "He replaced

the coffee he knocked out of her hand and wants to pay to clean her coat. Big deal."

The other angel pulled back to look at the sour face of the dark angel. "Where exactly did they transfer you from...?" Waiting for the other angel to fill in the name blank.

" ...Sid. Impossible dreams. Said I was not a real believer in dreams. I needed to lighten up."

"No kidding. Carmy here. Angel of Never-Ending Love. Well, Sid, start believing. These two people are going to fall madly in love with each other."

"Why?" A frown creased Sid's face. "They seemed perfectly happy with their lives as they are."

"They want a chance at love."

"How do you know that? Did they say that?"

"Didn't need to. It's in their hearts."

"You can see in their hearts?" Sid lowered his head looked at Carmy from the top of his eyes.

Carmy's sweet face looked back at Sid. "You can't?"

"Ms. Therriault? You are wanted in the conference room. Now."

Amy's piercing voice jerked Paige upright from her relaxing position, almost making her spill her coffee.

Just what I need. Another coffee stain on some part of my clothes.

Putting the cup down on her desk, she quickly gathered the file in front of her, dashed around her desk to her work station, picked-up her laptop, and gathered everything in her arms as she shouted. "I'm coming. I'm ready. I..." She stopped at the closed door and looked at her full hands.

The door swung open, there was Amy finishing her sentence. "...can't open the door?"

Paige brushed through hitting both sides of the door jam. "Thanks Amy. I owe you one."

Amy's voice followed her down the hall. "You owe me many, but who's counting."

Straightening her back, she entered the conference room with confidence and poise. Going straight to the front of the room, she offered greetings to the people she passed. Joining her design team at the front, together they sat up the presentation and prepared themselves.

Paige turned around to address the group when Mr. Smart and Mark Winston entered.

"People. This is our fearless leader's son, Mark Winston." Mr. Smart addressed the group.

Paige heard the "ahhhs" echo down the table. Keeping her composure, she nodded at the two men.

Mr. Smart directed his remarks in Paige's direction. "Paige, I heard you already bumped into Mark this morning."

With the emphasis on bumped, all heads turned to look at her. Swallowing hard, she cleared her throat to speak in an unwanted shaky, low voice.

"Yes, I did. Nice seeing you again, Mr. Winston."

"Mark, call me Mark." His deep, husky voice rolled over her. His smile was warm, but quite sexy.

Her design team stared at her.

Ruben raised one eyebrow and mouthed. "Mark?"

Shooting him her, 'don't start with me' look, she returned Mark's smile as graceful as she could.

Mr. Smart put his hands together. "Okay, people let's do your thing."

Paige and her group snapped to as if each rehearsed a part. They looked like a stage play, each presenting their piece of a giant puzzle. Paige tried not to look at Mark Winston, but her eyes kept going back to him. His attentive look and the smiles that wrinkled the corner of his eyes kept her just slightly off balance.

***

Carmy clapped his hands. "Oh, Sid. The sparks they are a flying."

"What sparks? They are in a room full of people. Several feet away from each other. She's giving a b-o-r-i-n-g, whatever it is she is doing." Sid huffed, crossed his arms over his chest.

Cocking his head, Carmy spread his arms wide. "You aren't feeling this? The magic? The beginning of a new love? You really are a hard-case."

Taking offense, Sid ground his teeth. "I am not a hard case. I am just lacking in some angel skills, that's all."

"Lacking?" Carmy released a deep belly laugh. Rocking back and forth he almost fell off the window ledge they were sitting on.

Dagger looks shot from Sid's eyes. "It's not that funny. Not all angels are created with this utopia outlook on life." Sadness crossed Sid's face. He turned his head to look at the panoramic view of the city.

Carmy stopped his laughing. He laid his hand on Sid's shoulder. "Sorry Bud. I just have never met an angel with such a bleak outlook and not believing that love is the answer."

Shaking his head, Sid looked back at the two people he was assigned to. "How can just love be the answer?" He turned to Carmy. "They seem happy enough to me."

Carmy looked at Mark and Paige. "That's the key word. They seem happy."

Sid and Carmy sat quietly watching their two charges.

***

Mark leaned his head back

against the high backed chair. Paige was a stunning looking woman. Not one of those high maintenance pencil-thin women. And spunky. He chuckled to himself thinking about their first meeting.

I liked spunk.

But it was her confidence in what she did that made her attractive.

Getting lost in the sound of her voice, the movement of her body, his mind wandered to thoughts of moonlight dinners, early morning coffee.

His dad asked if he would consider trying the work scene at the agency. Mark didn't have any real plans. After college he'd traveled, roamed around the world. Now he came home. Moving in with his Dad, his Mom died when he was a junior in college. Settling down was a thought that came very often. He vowed he had dated his last bimbo.

"Excellent work, people." Mr. Smart's voice brought Mark out of his thoughts. Seeing the beaming looks of satisfaction on the design team's face told him not only had he missed a superior presentation, but Paige was the star of the show. He stood up and clapped with the rest of the people in the room. Paige's face was glowing, but she also acknowledged her team.

For once he allowed himself to get lost in her electric blue eyes when their looks crossed and held.

CHAPTER TWO

"Is he not the most gorgeous specimen of a man you have ever seen?"

Paige just got back in her office, her back was to the door. Not even bothering to turn around to see who it was, the voice told it all.

Constance Payne.

Stacking her papers neatly on her work area, Paige pretended she was uninterested. "Who?"

Constance walked over to Paige's desk, propped herself on the edge. "Mark Winston."

"Is he not hot!" Amy's voice did make Paige turn around. Shaking her head at her assistant, Paige tilted it towards the overly styled woman occupying her office.

"And how do you know?" The condensing tone was unmistakable. Constance raised her perfectly arched eyebrow and narrowed a cold look at Amy.

Not breaking her stride, Amy laid a stack of envelopes and catalogs on Paige's desk. Standing behind Constance, Amy leaned over to say her words with accentuation so their meaning would be clear.

"He brought Paige coffee this morning." Target hit.

Constance glared at Paige.

Paige folded her arms across her chest and leaned against the ledge, rolling her eyes at Amy. The smug smile on Amy's face confirmed she made her point. Sauntering out of the office, her stride was one of great satisfaction.

If Paige could figure out a way to disappear, she would use it. Focusing slowly back to Constance, she could tell the woman was not pleased.

Constance Payne was a bitch on wheels. Always looking as if she just stepped off the pages of a magazine, she was the agency's in-charge person. The owners left her alone as long as she made them money and there were no complaints. Her way was "the" way and no one dared cross her. Never a real friend, she pretended to be a true pal to everyone. Just tolerating Constance was enough to keep Paige out of the woman's radar.

"He brought you coffee?" The tone carried the venom of a snake when stepped on. "So is that why you are to call him Mark?"

Summing up her words carefully, Paige shrugged her shoulders. "It was no big deal. He bumped into me and spilled my coffee so he replaced it. That's all."

Aware that Constance's eyes followed her, Paige went behind her desk and picked up the pile of mail Amy dumped. Acting as if it was an all consuming task, her eyes avoided contact with Constance's.

Rising slowly from her perch, Constance stood up, her hands on her hips, in what the office called the 'you better be straight with me' stance. Paige faced her head on, trying to keep the innocent look on her face. If Constance even thought she was being lied to, all hell would break loose.

Constance narrowed her eyes.

"That's it?"

"That's it. No big secret. Hardly worth mentioning. So I didn't." Time to change the subject. "So what about that presentation. My team did good, right?"

***

Sid readjusted his angel wings to lean back to get a good look at this new person in the scenario. "Who's the new broad?"

The two angels were on the edge of the window sill behind Paige's desk.

Carmy snickered. "Broad? What century are you from?"

The remark stung Sid's pride. He had been around awhile, but he loved the 1920's the best. But the cruelty of man against man hardened him. "Well, what would you call her?"

"An unnecessary intrusion." Carmy's sweet voice dripped with sarcasm.

The unusual tone made Sid snap his head around in alarm. "So what do we do? Is she going to screw up our mission? Oh, man. What do we do?" The panic rose up into his throat.

"Well first, 'we' calm down. This isn't

anything we can't handle. Do I detect a little bit of a feeling for our charges? " A wide grin spread across Carmy's face.

Sid shrugged his shoulders. "Well it is our assignment. And we can't help but want what is the best for them. Plus…" With his chest pumped out. "…I don't like this… woman."

The two angels sat in silence for a while watching the interaction between Paige and Constance. When Constance finally left, Paige swirled around in her office chair and watched out the window.

Sid saw the frown crease Paige's forehead. "Carmy, do you know what she is thinking?"

"Somewhat."

"So tell me."

"What do you think she is thinking?"

"That life is going to get complicated just when it seemed so settled."

Carmy patted Sid's shoulder. "Close, real close. You're learning."

***

Four o'clock was the time Paige decided she was done for the day. Her freshly cleaned trench coat reminded her of the morning incident and she really wanted to get out of the building before the rush. Mark Winston was an interesting man, but Paige was not willing to push for a relationship.

Let Constance have him. She is more into all the social stuff that would be required if I was to think it was possible to "date" Mark Winston. Date? There will be no dating.

Removing the plastic from her coat, she took it off the hanger and laid it across her forearm. Her messenger bag with her laptop stood upright ready to go. The rain stopped, the day turned sunny and Paige wanted to go outside and walk. She needed air.

As she opened her door, she informed Amy. "I am leaving. I worked all weekend on this project. I need a break."

Shifting her coat to her other arm. "By the way. Thanks for the help with Constance. You really like to poke the bear, don't you?"

Amy's shit-eating grin told it all. "I took great pleasure in that." She stood up and bowed.

Paige had to chuckle. "It was priceless. Okay, leaving. See you tomorrow." Her final words were thrown over her shoulder as she traveled down the rows of cubicles.

"Time it right and you may get lunch out of it tomorrow." Amy's words followed her. Paige waved her hand in the air.

No one was waiting for the elevator. Nodding to the girl at the reception desk, Paige was glad the doors opened as soon as she pushed the button. Entering the empty square box, she leaned against the wall and hit the down arrow.

Even the downstairs lobby was almost deserted. Paige pushed the heavy glass doors out and was hit in the face with a breath of fresh air. Putting on her sunglasses, she smiled and walked happily down the sidewalk towards her downtown apartment. Just this morning rain dampened her day and her spirits. Now she was feeling good.

***

Mark tried all day to get to Paige's office. His assistant, Brad, called Amy to be sure to get the right flavor of coffee, pick-up her coat and then delivered them both to her office.

Rounding the corner, he saw Amy gathering up her bag. Paige's office door was shut, the lights out. He stopped by Amy's desk, his hands in his pocket, his gaze on the darkened office.

"She gone?"

Amy's voice carried a touch of mischief as she spoke behind him. "Yes. Can I help you with something? Her phone number, address? Oh, but I'm sure Brad could get that for you."

His body turned around slowly, he let a grin spread over his face. "No, I just wanted to know if she got her coffee?"

"She did."

This was making him nervous. "Right kind?"

Amy folded her arms across her chest, stood with her weight on one leg. "Yes."

"Well..." He swung around looking back at the closed door. He wished he hadn't missed her. "...okay. I guess I'll catch her tomorrow."

Looking back around at Amy, her smug smile told him she was ready to play a matchmaking game.

Amy held her position and his focus. "If you timing is good."

Grinning, he turned to leave, pointing his index finger at her. "R i g h t."

"Mark."

Constance's high pitched voice made him cringe. "We're going out for drinks." She pouted her perfectly painted lips. "Say you'll come."

Mark would rather walk a mile in the snow than be held captive by this woman for the evening. "Sorry, Constance. I am calling it a day."

Her look was one of not going to press the subject, but...

Tom Winston came up behind her. "Going Mark?"

"Not tonight, Dad. Going home. See you there." Mark backed away from the two people in front of him. Twirling around, he spoke to Amy. "So I can count on you tomorrow to help me with 'my project'?"

"Absolutely." She grinned at a glaring Constance.

***

At home finishing some sketches on an ad campaign, Paige tried really hard not to think of Mark Winston. Her choice of music playing on the CD player was not helping. Slow and sexy, it brought her visions of hot sands and wild sex. Mexico. That must be it. She was preoccupied with the plans for Christmas.

Dinner. She picked up a meal for one from the deli. Her kitchen was compact and spotlessly clean. And why not? She didn't cook in it other than coffee. Propping up on one of her bar stools, she turned on the small TV on the counter. The news tragic, the weather a bleak forecast and sports, her team lost. Figures.

Two years ago she took the position at the agency. Fresh out of college, she kept her nose to the grindstone, finished top of her class. Loving design, her graphic job was rewarding and fulfilling.

She chuckled at some of the jerks she had dated. Now she was tired of the dating scene. Just crossing her mid-twenties mark, she wanted to have a family. Never did she want to be a career woman. Her goal was to be creative and give every aspect of life a chance.

Living alone had its moments, but sometimes she would like someone to go places with. Like dinner, a walk or just to talk.

Stretching, she took the plastic containers to the trash can.

Dinner done. Now what?

A hot bath, with lavender bubbles and a glass of a smooth, sweet wine was what she needed to end the day.

With her eye mask on, leaning back on her massaging bath pillow, the whirlpool jets and hot water created a warm fog. Her thoughts went to Mark Winston.

His tailor made expensive suit could not hide the firm torso of board shoulders and a tight chest. When he touched her, his arms were strong and inviting. A chill slipped down her stomach to her sweet place.

She let her body slip down into the swirling waters.

Damn it would be nice to feel that hardened body against me. I bet he's hot looking when naked.

Oh, go with it. I only have my fantasy. Mark Winston probably only wants women like Constance. Like I have a snowball's chance in hell of stroking that fabulous body. Every inch.

After the bath, she settled in her oversized bed and read a book by her favorite author. Getting lost in a love story would redirect her focus.

Not happening.

***

Mark drove to his childhood home in the country on Ewing Lake. Parking his car in the same spot in the garage he had since high school, entering the same door, throwing his keys in the same bowl brought a sigh from him. Loosening his tie, he went to the kitchen and found dinner the housekeeper left. Alone in the huge house, he was nevertheless comfortable. It was home.

Taking a glass out of the cupboard, he picked up his plate, silverware and went to the den. Placing everything on the coffee tables, he flipped on the TV, sat down and picked at his food.

Nothing on the tube interested him. Visions of Paige kept crossing his mind. Like making love on a beach. Her long auburn hair entangled in his fingers.

Enough.

Going back into the kitchen he opened the fridge and took out a cold beer. Settling back down, he finished watching the news and was not interested in the TV tabloid show.

Paige. Strong, confident and oh so sexy.

A shower would calm down all those erotic feelings. Leaning against the shower wall he could feel his desire rise as well as his manhood.

No, Paige was no bimbo. She was a flesh and blood woman.

He turned the water temperature to cool.

His bed welcomed his over stimulated body. He could not get the possibility of Paige someday sharing it with him out of his mind.

***

"These two are like watching paint dry." Sid was pacing around the ceiling of Mark's room.

Carmy nodded. "That's why we were assigned to them."

"Since when did boring lives become an assignment?"

Carmy smiled his all knowing smile. "Since we were sent a request."

"A request? Who put in a request? Boring People R us? What? Are they not boring enough for the group?"

The cute angel laughed a deep belly laugh. "You know Sid, sometimes your dry humor is really funny."

Frowning, Sid snapped back. "I'm not trying to be funny. Why these two?"

"Why not?" Carmy sat back on his wings. "Someone wants them happy."

"Duh. Everybody wants somebody happy. What is so special about these two?" Sid and Carmy were walking outside of Mark's house.

Carmy put his arm over Sid's shoulder. "We don't question the orders. We just make sure the request is answered."

Sid kept in step with Carmy. "And why is that?"

"Because that is our job and we love our work."

Sid just grunted.

CHAPTER THREE

The alarm clock started with a soft classical tune. Paige was partial to waking up to calm music, to stretch and feel the start of the day hover over her. A crack of dawn person, it was five a.m. and the first thing she did every day was run. Since it was fall in Wisconsin, the mornings were crisp and fresh. Perfect.

In her sweats and t-shirt, her long hair in a pony tail pulled through the back of a baseball cap, she bounced down the front steps of her loft apartment. Running was a way to get her juices going. To plan her day, set her ideas for new projects, avoiding Mark Winston.

Her pace stopped short.

Where did that come from? I thought I finished all that last night.

Her hands on her hips, she stood in the middle of the sidewalk, looking at her watch, five-thirty. If she cut her run short, she could get to the office before anyone else. If she arrived earlier than anyone else, she could hide out in her office. Therefore avoiding a chance meeting in the lobby or elevator with Mark Winston.

That's the plan.

It took her no time to get back to her home and jump in the shower. Lathering up she plotted her plan.

Grab my coffee. It opens at six.

Get up to my office, to my desk. Walla, done deal.

Dressed and ready to go, she walked briskly to her coffee shop.

The young kid behind the counter was surprised to see her there so early. "Miss Therriault. You're up and at it early."

"Yes, Joe. Getting a jump start today."

Paige tapped her finger nails on the counter. Her adrenalin was pumped.

A mission.

To steer clear of the man who

makes my knees weak.

The coffee cup was placed in front of her nervous hand. Laying a bill on the counter.

"Keep the change." She snatched the hot cup with her gloved hand.

She bolted for the door, pushing it open with her hip. The one block left to go was done at a brisk stride. Her long legs banished the distance quickly.

The lobby was empty except for the security guard, Randal. In his white uniform, the slender older man was always there when she arrived and there when she left.

Did the man have a home?

He tipped his hat. "Good morning, Ms. Therriault. You're early today. Have a good day."

"Yes, you too." She waved as she breezed by. Pressing the elevator button for up, she squirmed as she kept glancing around. When the doors opened it was empty.

Thank goodness.

As it rose passed the many floors it took to reach her floor, she prayed the doors wouldn't open at any of the other floors. Then a familiar scent assaulted her nose. It was Mark's and the way he felt standing next to her yesterday, his hand lightly at her back.

Damn. Where did that come from? Impossible. That was almost twenty-four hours ago.

A ding brought her mind back as the doors slid open. Poking her head out first, she was relieved the receptionist wasn't even at her desk. Stepping fully out, she strolled down the hall, amused at all the empty desks including Amy's. Her keys jingled as she balanced her cup, bag and purse to unlock the door. Throwing her stuff on the desk, she was careful not to spill her coffee. A sigh of relief escaped her lips as she sat down in her chair and swirled towards the window.

Mission accomplished.

***

Sid yawned and stretched his arms. His wing unfolded and extended out. "What is she doing? We didn't need to come on duty until eight. Now we are at the office and it's six-thirty."

Blond angel was studying Paige. Leaning his head to the side, he intently watched her face. "She's avoiding her feelings."

Lowering his wings, Sid tilted his head to the side. "What feelings?"

"Her feelings." Carmy smacked Sid's arm. "She is attracted to Mark, but is afraid to let the feelings be real."

Rubbing his arm, Sid glared at the other angel. "Why? If people have feelings for each other they should just…"

"…just what. Spill their heart all over the floor?"

"Well that sounds rather dramatic. Just spit out what they think." Sid took on a smug look.

Carmy shook his head. "She can't. It hurt her when her parents divorced. She doesn't trust love ever after. She just wants to get married and have kids."

"What about love?" Sid couldn't believe he was saying such a cheesy phrase.

Carmy propped his head in his hands. "What indeed."

Enraged, Sid stood up, marched up and down the window still. "So she isn't planning on loving her husband? Just marrying him?

How stupid. That's ridiculous. You can't do that."

Carmy kept his focus on Paige. A frown creased his brow. "Well you can, and lots of people do. But I want better for Paige."

The pacing stopped. Sid stood on the edge, frowning also. "So do I. What are we going to do?" He turned to face Carmy. "Tell me our next step."

"Well," Carmy started. "I don't know."

Sid spread his legs apart, put his hands on his hip. "You don't know? How can you not know? You are the angel of Never-Ending Love. You know how to do this. Don't you?"

"I'm working on a plan. Give me some space."

Flapping his wings, Sid soared to the panel of windows that showed the hallway. "Well space is getting tight. Here come the troops, including that annoying person, Constance."

***

Proud of his timing, at seven-thirty, Mark pulled open the glass doors at the coffee shop, sure he was ahead of Paige. Ordering a large, black coffee, he sat down at a vacant table for two and glued his gaze to the door. He expected her any minute.

Ten minutes passed eight he knew he missed her. Tossing his empty cup into the trash, he shoved the glass door harder than he meant to, but...

Damn where is she?

The ride up the elevator was slow and long. At his floor he shuffled through the crowd of people, exchanging greetings with the people as he passed. At his office, Brad was already at his desk.

Spotting Mark, he jumped up and gathered the messages. "Here you are. Coffee?"

Mark took the slips of paper, without looking at them. " No, I've had my coffee. Is Paige Therriault here today?"

"I'll find out and get it to you asap."

Mark went into his office without a word.

***

Brad dialed Amy's extension. "Is your boss there?"

Amy's voice was muffled. Brad

figured it was because she was moving around. "Yes. She was here before me. Why?"

"Mark asked."

Amy lowered her voice. "No kidding. What do you think is going on?"

"Don't have a clue. You?" Brad cupped his hand around the phone.

"No. Call you back." Amy hung up.

Brad went into Mark's office. "She came in early. Must have some project going, or work to do..." His voice faded.

Mark shrugged. "Okay."

Brad stood for a moment.

Mark looked up at him. "Yes?"

"Nothing. Ah, anything else?" Brad still hadn't moved.

"Your work that needs to be done?"

Brad pointed his index finger. "Right. On it." He departed.

***

Amy arranged her desk for the day while keeping an eye on Paige, who was bent over her work station laptop. Half an hour later, she took ten morning messages, finished Paige's appointments for the day and was ready to do the lunch order. Brad was still waiting for her explanation as to why their bosses did not run into each other.

Laying the messages on Paige's desk, Amy started rattling off a list of things to do. Talking to Paige's back, she was ready to take the lunch order.

"So what is for lunch today? Sushi? Metro? Deli?

"It's a working lunch. We have that covered." At the sound of Mark's rich voice, Paige twirled around on her stool.

Amy, with her pen in mid-air smiled. Mr. McGorgeous was leaning against the door jam, his drop dead sexy smile highlighting his tan, perfectly sculptured face.

Paige shot a look at Amy. "Was that on my schedule?"

Amy put her pen in her mouth, winked at Mark. "Oh, my mistake. Here it is right here. 'Working lunch'. Silly me asking you about a lunch order."

Stunned as to what to comeback with, Paige nodded at Mark. "Okay then, lunch in...?

"...board room." Prying his tall body from the doorway.

Amy secretly thumbed up as she walked by. "Nice."

***

Mark lifted his eyes as members of the agency marched in like obedient soldiers. He got to the board room before even the caterer got there. Finishing up some work, he wanted to observe how each person entered. Body language was a big part in how a person worked and got along with others.

The caterer, from the deli down the street, arrived at eleven-thirty. A long table was set up as a buffet style lunch. An eye appealing lay-out, the servers were ready to go by eleven-fifty.

The early arrivers started coming in at eleven-fifty-five. Mark sat back as he separated them into groups. The 'want to get to the food first' group started filling their plates, piling it high. Then there was 'kiss the boss' ass group'. They filtered in securing their place at the table before anyone else.

For the next five minutes he

observed, calculating the behavior of the staff.

The Ad Exec sat together. Dressed impressively, they were the front line. Get the account. Only two remained faithful to the company. The other five were young hot shots using this job as a stepping stone, as had many before them. Fun guys, good to have a drink with, go to a hockey game, but nothing lasting. Mark watched them blather back and forth as they got their food.

The heads of other departments filtered in. Mark sat back as Paige and her associate director, Ruben entered. Picking their spot at the other end, his eyes followed them as they got their plates, chatting as if they were best friends. As Paige sat her plate down, she scanned the table. Stopping when she noticed Mark, she nodded slightly, looked over at Ruben and sat down. Ruben's perception was sharp as his eyes darted between the two.

Mark would be jealous, but Ruben was gay. What Mark did envy was the friendship the two shared. Paige was relaxed around Ruben, while with him she seemed tense and on guard. Their heads together, the two spoke quietly. Whether business or personal, Mark didn't know. But Ruben made her smile. Mark wanted to make her smile. Her smiles were quite sexy. They lit up her eyes, her shoulders relaxed.

Yes, I want to make her smile.

The slight chuckle from Paige was the first he had heard or seen. He could feel the joy of hearing it in his chest.

His thoughts were interrupted by the arrival of the Executive Board, Tom Winston, Jim Bradley, Allan Smart, and, of course, Constance. Her phony greeting and overzealous smile made him rotate in his chair. Constance was not part of the original three partners. She had joined the firm after he entered college. Relief, his Dad sat next to him was short lived as Constance took the seat on his other side.

Mark grew up with the Bradleys and the Smarts. The agency always existed in his lifetime. Growing up with the partners' kids was his childhood. His best friend and college roommate was Jim's oldest son, Jim Jr. He dated Allan's middle daughter, Sara, in high school. Nothing serious, in fact he attended her wedding a few years ago. What Mark felt sitting at this table in this room with these men, were his roots. Where he belonged. Where he wanted to stay.

"People, let's get started." Standing up, Allan's voice brought a quiet to the room, pausing long enough to get everyone's awareness. "We have a big announcement."

Now the people were quiet.

Continuing. "As you all should know by now, Mark Winston is now a member of the firm as a Junior Partner. We welcome him into the fold as a major asset. And being the boss' son didn't hurt."

A faint chuckle and polite applause echoed around the table. Except for Constance, she clapped like she was at a rock concert. Mark was glad she didn't do a 'Woo hoo'.

"And..." pausing for effect. "...we have a new account. A major account. Ben Olson." A gasp was heard in unison around the table.

"Yes, folks, he is expanding his line to include shoes, apparel and jewelry in addition to his signature 'For Male' cologne."

The chatter level rose. Mark watched Paige and Ruben. They both were pleased with the news. He watched the exchange between them with a sly smile.

Allan directed his attention to the design team. "Paige. You have the ad campaign. I know you will do me proud, you always do."

Paige mouthed 'thank you'. Ruben was hardly able to hold in his excitement.

"And…" Allan turned to Mark. "Mark will be the project manager. I expect you two to work very closely together."

Mark kept his eyes on Paige. Her quick look at him, the slight nod said it all. She was surprised, but had no idea it was his suggestion. Being the good Art Director she was, she would do as she was instructed.

Working with her would keep his body awake at night. Every since she walked, well fell into his life, he was captured. There was something that made him think all this was designed.

Destiny.

Not a big believer. But still there was something.

Allan clapped his hands once in a pep clap. "Okay, folks. This is a major coup d'état for our company. We need the best all of you have. Bring it."

The group at the table stood up and started talking all at once. Mark stood, shook hands with his father and the rest of the executive board. Constance's hand shake was the hardest to get free of.

When he turned to go to Paige, Constance blocked his way. "Oh, Mark. How exciting. Project manager. You know if you need me for anything, I am here."

Trying to shift her out of his way, he put his hands on her arms to shuffle her aside. Over her shoulder he saw Paige leave with Ruben.

Constance was still talking. "You know we could plan over dinner..."

"Sorry, I've got plans for tonight."

"Tomorrow?"

"Can't say. Will you excuse me?"

She grabbed his arm as he tried to pull away. Her death grip on him was hard to pry off. "Well, we must get together. For business, of course."

"We will." Finally, he was free, but Paige was gone.

***

The angels sat crossed legged in the empty board room in the middle of the conference table.

"They have to work 'closely' together." Carmy bounced up and down, clapping his hands.

Sid isn't jumping for joy. "Did you see Constance? She is getting on my last nerve."

"Yes, she is a problem. We need to get her assigned somewhere else."

The idea appealed to Sid. "Like where? Japan? Russia?"

"They don't have an agency in Russia?"

"Perfect, she can start one. How do we get that done?"

"We don't. We are assigned to Mark and Paige. Not Constance."

Sid leapt to his feet. "But she is interfering with our work."

"Still not our problem. We have to do

this with the obstacles we encounter."

Sid huffed as he sat back down. "I wouldn't call her an 'obstacle'."

"And what, pray tell, would you call her?"

Sid rocked back on his butt. "A bitch that is in my way."

CHAPTER FOUR

Mark was going to get it right this time. Up at four a.m., he was waiting at the coffee shop as the owner unlocked the doors at six.

"Good morning, sir. Up and at it this fine morning."

Being pleased with his foresight, he knew she had not been here yet. The young clerk behind the counter was waiting for his order.

"A large black and strong." Mark kept his eyes on the door. Without really looking, he paid for the coffee and took a seat facing the door.

It was only about a minute when she jerked the door open. Then stopped dead in her tracks. Her eyes were wide with surprise. Shuffling her bag from one hand to the other, she finally greeted him.

"Mr. Winston." The stutter in her voice let him know he flustered her.

Leaning back, he noticed her body language in the defense mode. Rigid torso, shoulders stiff, arms taut, hands in a semi-fist,

This girl is going to give me a work-out.

This made him all the more fascinated with her. He liked a little chase.

This is one serious woman. And oh so hot!

"Mark." He smiled as he corrected her.

Breaking her stance, she continued on to the counter. Her back to him. "Yeah, well about that."

He moved up behind her. "What about that?" His words brought her around sharply.

Her eyes locked on his and it took her a few seconds to respond. "I...think...we should keep it professional."

In a casual, relaxed way he leaned on the counter. "And what is not professional about Mark? If you keep calling me Mr. Winston I will think you are talking to my Dad."

Now he had her attention. Her

eyes shot sparks. Stepping back like she was going to throw a punch, her words hit the mark. "Look, 'Mr.-I –am-the-boss'-son-and-damn-good-looking', I don't fish off the company pier."

Mark stood up straight. "What fish? I am just trying to be friendly. What does that mean anyway?"

Grabbing up her cup, Paige turned and headed for the door. Mark beat her by one second. Pushing the door open for her, he caught her scorching look as she swept by. Following her, he had to speed up his pace.

How do women walk so fast in those shoes?

Finally, at the entrance of their building, she was stopped by a surge of people. Almost to her, a couple of men block his way, putting him back behind the line for the elevator. Trying to wedge his way up to her, he barely got in the elevator as the doors shut. Readjusting his position to look around, Mark found Paige in the corner, watching him. With the patience of a saint he waited until the elevator was empty except for the two of them, before he approached her. His back hit the rear wall next to her.

Looking over at her, he chuckled. "Fishing off the company pier? Seriously?"

Paige broke into laughter. "I'm sorry. Can we forget about this? I think I am over reacting."

"How about this? We are co-workers and friends?" His body turned to face her. Paige's pose changed to welcoming, he continued. "I'm just new and I like your style." His eyes traveled to her breast, then he jerked them back up. "Of work, professional of course"

Paige held out her hand. "Agreed."

With her soft hand in his he ran his thumb over her skin.

When the bell rang and the doors opened, still holding hands, they turned around to see the disapproving look on Constance's face.

***

Carmy is flitting around like a firefly. "They are getting closer. Just going to take some time, but,,," His words hung in mid-air. He swarmed around Constance. "...what is she doing here?" Holding out his arms, he addressed his question to Sid.

Moving slower than molasses in winter, Sid adjusts his eyes to see what stopped Carmy's joyful onslaught of words. Constance Payne was glaring at Mark and Paige. Paige jerked her hand out of Mark's and bolted towards her office.

Mark watched her go with a slight smirk on his face. Turning towards Constance, he gave her a wiry grin.

"Good morning, Ms. Payne. Lovely morning isn't it?" Whistling, he strolled passed her and down the hall to his office.

Constance was left standing with her hands on her hip and her eyes full of anger.

Sid fluttered around her. "I think the woman is pissed."

Carmy clapped his hands. "She is isn't she?"

"So where are we going?" Sid growled. "And why are these two getting up before the crack of dawn? When is the weekend? What day is this?"

Already on his way towards Paige, Carmy pointed Sid towards Mark. "Link up within the hour."

Carmy zigzagged over the offices and cubicles with a happy melody following him.

Sid flew slowly and a little sluggish down the hallway to the executive offices trying not to bump into the walls. Not that they would hurt him. He just would lose his bearings and have to rethink where he was going. No happy song followed him. More like the Funeral March-dum- dum-de-dum-dum-de-dum.

**

At seven o'clock Amy came up on the elevator. She saw Mark and Paige get on at the same time. She so wanted her boss to date a hot man. Paige was a dream to work for, consistent, professional and kind. But she carried a wedge of sadness in her eyes and a small chip on her shoulder.

Embarking the elevator, Amy was surprised to see Mark and Paige going in different directions. Constance was stomping down another hall towards her office.

What the hell happened on the ride up?

Rushing to get to her desk she

could see that Paige was in the office already. As she hung up her coat and purse, she kept her eyes on her boss. Paige's body movement was not her normal tense, but more relaxed like she enjoyed the morning commute.

Powering on the computer, Amy shuffled papers to find some reason to go to Paige's office.

Oh what the hell. I'm a nosey bitch and I am going in.

"Paige, how was your walk to work? Run into anybody?" Amy breezed in like she had a purpose.

Paige looked up from the paper she was writing. A look of confusion crossed her eyes. "No. Nothing out of the norm. Walked to work, got my coffee, rode up with Mark Winston." The look of wiry wit was not wasted on Amy.

"Really? So do tell." Amy's glee could not be contained.

Paige leaned back in her chair. "What's to tell? We are co-workers, and now friends."

"That's it? Oh, come on." Amy was bent over the desktop, thirsty for some juicy gossip.

"That's it. Now go to work. I have a new project to start. Call my design team. I reserved the conference room for two this afternoon. Tell them to bring their drawing pads and creative ideas."

Amy was not ready to let go of this subject yet. Straightening up, she asked with an edge in her voice. "Should I invite Mark?"

Paige snickered. "Why would you do that? Does he draw?"

"Fine, we will get to business as usual. Anything else? Boss." Amy added a bit of snarkyness to her voice.

"No that will be all. Thank you." Paige dismissed her.

Trudging out, Amy tossed the pad and pencil on her desk. Hands on her hips, she twisted around to look back at Paige.

Paige's head was down.

Something happened. And I will find out what.

***

The two angels reconnected in the break room by the coffee machine.

Carmy was sitting on the counter when Sid flew in. "So how is he?"

"Happy." Sid landed next to Carmy. "Her?"

Carmy nodded. "Not unhappy."

Sid folded his arms as he fluttered in front of Carmy." So what is your next step?"

"Our next step." Carmy looked down.

Sid flew a little closer. "Okay ,what's our next plan."

"You come up with something." Carmy was out of ideas.

"Well, Paige and her Mom are going to dinner tonight."

"And…?"

"We get Mark to go to the same restaurant."

Carmy leaned back. "Sid, old buddy that is a great idea. You been holding out on me?"

Sid looked down at his feet. "No, I have my moments. I have been an angel for awhile now."

Carmy leaned forward. "How long of a while?"

"Is that really important?" Sid wanted to avoid the subject.

Carmy refused to give it up. "Yes, it is.

What are you hiding?"

"Nothing. I am just trying to do good on this assignment." Sid settled on the table, begging with his eyes for Carmy to stop asking questions.

"Why is this one so important?" Carmy flew to his friend's side.

A tear rolled down the dark angel's cheek. "If I mess up, I will be assigned to the Angel of Death."

Shocked, Carmy put his arm around Sid. "We won't let that happen. We'll get these two together. I promise."

The frown that creased Sid's face said it all. "Why do you want to make sure I don't get sent away?"

Rising up on the air, Carmy lingered over Sid. "I like you Sid. Even your dark, cynical side. You and I need to show them we can do this."

Jumping to his feet on the counter, Sid hovered in the air also.

"We can do this. " Pounding on his chest, Sid shouted. "We are the Angels of Never-Ending Love."

Bringing his hands down on Sid's

shoulder, Carmy held the fluttering angel down. "Whoa boy, we need to keep a low profile. We don't need the High Angels thinking we have lost control."

Sid's wings went down to his side; he took a jock's stance. "Right, we're cool."

***

Mark strolled over toward Paige's office as soon as he saw her and her group in the conference room. Slinking up to Amy's desk, he pressed his back against the cubical wall; spoke out of the side of his mouth.

"Got anything to use to my advantage?"

Without looking up, Amy kept typing. "Dinner. Tonight. With her Mother."

Surprised he turned around and rested his chin on the top of the wall. "Really? Where?"

"Diego's"

"Mexican." He bit his lower lip. "I know the place. Time?"

"They usually meet around six-thirty."

"Okay. Thanks."

"No problem."

Making a bee-line for his father's office, Mark leaned in and saw his father sitting at his computer, his back to the door. Entering quietly, Mark stood behind him.

"Hey, Dad."

The elder Winston swirled around. "Hey, kid, what's new?"

Knowing how much his father wanted him in the company, Mark was glad of his decision. "Wondering if you'd like to go out to dinner tonight?" Then as an afterthought. "Just us two."

His dad's smile was instantly recognizable as approval. "Hey, that's an excellent idea. Where to? I know a great steak…"

Cutting off his father's words. "…I was thinking Mexican?"

"Well, there's several…"

"How about Diego's?"

"Diego's is good. Seven?"

"Make it six-fifteen."

Tom Winston narrowed his eyes. "Fine. Six-fifteen."

Mark looked out the window at the bright sunshine streaming through the floor to ceiling glass windows.

Done deal.

***

Diego's was an upscale authentic Mexican café. The walls were covered with an Aztec theme, the bar was welcoming and full this time of day. Young, up-and-coming business people networking.

Having walked the few blocks from work to the restaurant, Paige waited on the bench in the lobby watching the people socialize. Her mother, always fashionably late, but since the divorce a transformation had taken place. No longer was she the mundane wife of a well-connected businessman. She was now an extraordinary woman in her own right. When the glass doors swung opened a classy, chic woman breezed in. Turning heads of both male and female, her striking beauty bedazzled all. Dressed expensively, but tasteful, her entrance always bought a smile to Paige.

As her mother crossed the distance between them, Paige met her half-way. Kissing her cheek, Paige's mom's bouquet of expensive perfume surrounded her.

"Mom."

"Daughter."

Looping theirs arms, Paige guided her mother to the reservation desk. The hostess greeted her as a steady customer.

"Ms. Paige. Your table is ready." Following the young woman in the all black uniform, never really looking around. Trekking through the maze of tables, she was startled when a man stepped up in front of her.

"Ms. Therriault." The familiar voice made her look up.

Mark Winston.

Blocking her way, she saw no way around other than knocking him over. She glanced at the other man sitting at the table.

Shit. Tom Winston.

Her mother's voice sounded behind her. "Pagie, darling, who is this handsome young man?"

Paige stepped back and turned sideways. Her voice was not her usual 'in control voice'. "Mom, this is Mark Winston and his father Tom Winston. They own the agency where I work."

Tom Winston stood up at the introduction.

Paige continued. "This is my mother, Vivian Therriault."

Mark put his hand on the small of Paige's back, gently moving her back as their parents shook hands. She glanced at his profile, he looked straight ahead.

How did this happen?

Diverting her eyes back to her mom and Tom Winston, she was taken aback by the obvious attraction between the two.

Mark's voice echoed in her ear. "Would you two lovely women join us for dinner?"

As Paige opened her mouth to object, Vivian sat down next to Tom. "We'd love to."

Mark pulled out a chair next to him and offered it to Paige. Caught in a trap, Paige, with all the poise she could muster, sat down.

Her legs brushed against Mark's. It was like an electric charge. Moving her chair slightly to the left, she stopped when he put his arm on the back of her chair. Leaning into her, his low voice vibrating against her neck.

"They seem to be getting along."

Paige looked at Vivian and Tom.

Her mother was lifting a glass of wine, clinking it on Tom's. Her face actually shining.

"Yes. Did you plan this?" Turning sharply, her nose touched his cheek.

When he turned to face her, their lips almost touching. "No. It must be fate."

***

"Fate? Is he kidding?" Sid shouted out his angry words.

Carmy rested in the plants that outlined the tables. "What is your problem? We wanted them to accidently meet tonight."

Sid fluttered over the ivy. "Yes, but he is taking credit for our plan."

Carmy leaned back, watching the four. "So?"

"Well, I came up with the idea. I put it in his head to go over to Amy's desk." Sid snapped his hands to his waist.

"And does he know that?" Carmy was enjoying watching the situation unfold at the table.

That stopped Sid fluttering. "No."

Carmy answered without looking at

Sid. "Does he know about us?"

Sid looked sheepishly at Carmy. "Well. No."

"Then what does it matter?"

Shamefacedly, Sid sighed. "I guess it doesn't, but…"

"We do this for love, Sid. Remember that." Carmy put his hands behind his head, reclined back.

Sid looked around. "Are other angels here?"

"No. Why?"

"Well, Mom and Pop are sure into each other. Who's working their case?"

"Not everyone needs help. Some people do it on their own."

"Really? Are they falling in love?"

"Well maybe later. Right now they are just horny for each other."

The shock radiated over Sid. "Carmy? What kind of an idea is that for an angel to have?"

"The right idea. If those two decide to fall in love, they won't need any help. They will do it on their own."

***

As the dinner ended, the men walked the women outside. Vivian lived in the opposite direction of Paige and quite a distance. As the group sauntered down the sidewalk, Vivian wandered over to the curb where a shiny black Lexus was parked. Hugging her daughter first, Vivian shook Mark's hand then hugged Tom. They spoke in low tones to each other as Paige and Tom shuffled their feet, looking anywhere but at each other.

As Vivian's tail lights faded away, Tom stood with his hands in his pocket for an uncomfortable amount of time. Finally, he turned to the couple.

"Paige. Thanks for an enjoyable evening. Your mother is charming."

Paige nodded. "Totally not my doing, but it was a nice evening. Thank you."

Tom turned to Mark. "Son, if you orchestrated this, well done, conductor."

Paige turned sharply to look at Mark. "You said you didn't plan this?"

"No..." He held up his hands. "...I didn't plan this. It just happened." He turned to his Dad. "Thanks Dad, but this was not orchestrated as you implied."

"Whatever you say, son." Socking Mark on the shoulder. "My car's in the lot over here. Want a ride back to the office lot, Mark?"

Mark shook his head. "No. Nice night, I'll walk."

Tom smiled. "See you two in the morning at work." With his hands still in his pockets, he walked away humming.

Mark started to talk uncontrollably. "Honest, Paige. I did not plan for our parents to meet. But I think it's a good thing. Dad's lonely. Vivian seems like a lot of fun. Do you agree?"

No answer, just a look.

"Disagree?" Mark was trying to get a smile.

Then she laughed. "No it's a good thing. Mom needs some companionship. Tom is a good man. At least I don't have to do a background check."

Turning in unison, Mark looked at Paige. "Where is your car?"

"I live within walking distance of

work, just down the street."

They walked together in the direction of Paige's apartment.

Side by side they traveled down the sparsely lit sidewalk. The trees were covered with small twinkling lights, the street lamps a soft muted glow. The late fall night was chilly, but clear and fresh.

"So what does your mother do?" Mark started the feeble conversation.

Paige chuckled. "You mean besides trying to map out my life?"

"What do you mean?" Mark's interest was honest.

Paige touched the dry leaf on a tree. It came off in her hand. "Mom can be a bit overbearing. My folk's break-up was messy. So she pursues me to be hers. A pissed woman and a pompous man make for bad feelings."

"I see. Do you see your father?"

Mark heard a hint of anger as she answered. "No. He's remarried. Has a new life. My Mom has a chain of bookstores. The Mystery Cranny."

"She owns them? I've been there. I go all the time. I enjoy a good mystery."

Paige stopped while Mark continued a few steps. When he realized she was no longer next to him, he turned around to look for her.

"This is where I live."

Mark walked back, stopped and looked up. "Nice."

Paige held out her hand. "Thanks for walking me home.

Mark took her hands in both of his. "For friends, I'd say this was a perfect evening."

Paige nodded. "Yes. Good night." He slid his hands off hers. She turned towards the door. He continued on down the sidewalk.

CHAPTER FIVE

"Paige, Mr. Mark Winston has set up a meeting with you in his office at ten." Amy's voice echoed over the intercom on Paige's phone.

"Thank you, Amy." Paige couldn't help but notice the touch of excitement in her assistant's voice.

Paige was comfortable about meeting with Mark. After their dinner, she accepted being on just friendly terms. Never mind that he made her stomach curl when he honed in on her with those steel gray eyes. Or that an innocent brush of his hand or body started an electric surge in her breast. Those were her problems. Not dating at work was a rule she would live by.

My rule. My world.

Glancing at her watch showed nine forty-five. She needed to finish up one last minute change before walking on down to his office.

This was a big campaign. A major marketer was expanding his line. Ideas floated around in her head since made aware of the assignment. Many rough sketches were ready to present to Mark. It surprised her he wanted to be the project manager, but maybe this was his way of paying his dues so that people took him seriously.

Five till, she gathered up her presentation. As she walked out the door, Amy met her.

"Let's see." Amy turned Paige around. Paige wore one of her basic work outfits. Taupe suit, sensible matching heels. Her hair was long, so she let it flow over her shoulders naturally. Amy brushed at the back of her suit coat, turned her around, straightened her overly starched white collared shirt. "You really need to get some color in your wardrobe."

Paige shook Amy off. "It never seemed to bother you before."

"Oh, it's always bothered me, just didn't see any need to bring it up before now."

"So, why is it important now?"

"Because there is a hot hunk of a man lurking around that wants you bad."

"Don't be ridiculous. Mark and I are just friends. Co-workers."

Amy stood back with a hand on her hip. "Who said it was Mark?"

Crap!

"I'm leaving." Turning around sharply, Paige marched towards Mark's office.

The closer she got, the more an exciting, tingling feeling swept over her. Thinking she had the best of both worlds, Paige could allow feeling hot and bothered on the inside about Mark, but cool and friendly on the outside.

What do they call that? Unrequited love? Works for me.

Entering his office, she was struck by how handsome he always looked. He had removed his suit jacket, rolled up his sleeves revealing strong, hard forearms. The mid-morning sunlight made his sun-streaked hair shine. Still in its immaculate style, she so wanted to ruffle it up.

This man is too perfect. He needs

to get a little dirty.

"Mark. I am really excited about this project."

He looked up at her. Laying down his pen, his drop dead smile made her weak in the knees. He stood up. "Good. This will be a good thing for the agency." Motioning to the table. "Let's see what you have, Paige."

Spreading out her papers, she was aware of his nearness. He always smelled so good. His shoulder brushed hers as he leaned in to look.

"Nice. Explain the concept."

Paige put on her glasses and moved away from him. It was too hard to concentrate with him so close.

***

Sid and Carmy sat on an empty spot on the table.

"Look at them. Talking and inconspicuously touching. This is good." Carmy's aura is all aglow.

Angling his head, Sid is confused. "So this goes on for how long?"

"Awhile."

"Seems like this is taking forever."

"Baby steps, Sid. Baby steps."

"This gets any slower and they will be dead from old age."

"Patience my good angel. These things take time."

"And I thought Impossible Dreams took a long time." Sid looked over the drawings. "She's a good artist."

"Yes, she has a lot of talents she keeps on a low key."

"Like what else?"

"She cooks like a chef. Sings like a nightingale. And is hot in bed..."

Sid held up his hand. "Stop! Too much information." Squinting at Carmy. "I don't even want to know how you know that."

***

After a long week at work, Paige took Sunday to be alone. Sleeping late, she ran around the trail and ended at a favorite breakfast/brunch café. The coffee was rich and full-bodied, she savored her second cup as she read the paper. Paige was satisfied with how her life was. Sure she wanted marriage and kids, but there were a few years before her bio clock sounded the alarm.

Walking back, she thought of

where she was in her plan. Her job was her dream job. It was challenging, creative and demanding in a good way. When it consumed her, it was a good rush. Then every once in a while it gave her a break.

But this was not one of those times. Mark wanted the power point presentation done this week. Friday at the latest. Before the Thanksgiving holidays. Her team was right on it. It was going to be great. No, today was okay to take a break. Tomorrow she would hit the floor running.

Stepping up the approach to her brownstone loft, she remembered she had a chick flick. A big drop of rain hit her in the eye. Looking up she saw the dark clouds rolling over. Ducking inside, she was glad she went for a run in the morning.

***

The racket ball came at Mark fast and hard. His brother Richard was an expert at hand ball. Home for a few weeks, Richard, married with two kids, lived in Maine. Back for Thanksgiving, he and Mark were spending some guy time together.

Mark missed.

Richard laughed at his brother's mistake. "Got your mind on something else? A girl maybe?"

"Maybe."

Richard grabbed the bouncing ball. "Do tell?"

"Nothing to tell. She won't date co-workers."

"She's at the agency? Don't tell me she's that superficial broad that is as phony as shit?"

"Constance Payne? Oh, hell no. Paige, she's the Art Director."

"And she's not having any part of you, lil' bro?"

"No, that's not totally true. We're friends."

"Oh, man she's playing the 'friend card'? You're shit out of luck, dude."

"Don't count me out yet."

Richard came over and put his arm around Mark's shoulder. "She makes you hot?"

Together they walked out of the court. Mark chuckled. "Yes, she makes me hot."

"So what are you going to do?"

"See if I can convince her to be more than friends."

"Good luck with that. For now, take lots of cold showers."

"Thanks for the advice."

***

"Okay, what we have here is a failure to communicate." Carmy is setting on the hood of Mark's car as he and Richard drive home.

On the top, his legs hanging against the windshield, Sid looked perplexed. "You think?" Sid leaned forward. "So what are we going to do?"

"Well I still think a plan to get them together in Mexico is good."

Sid nodded. "Okay, how do we do that?"

Carmy leaned back. "We have to get Paige to tell Mark. Then we can get the wheels of his brain twirling."

"We can do that?"

"Sid ole' buddy. We have lots of ways to get people to do what we want. And the funny thing is they think it is all their idea."

"Yeah, I learned that during that dinner." Sid took a deep breath. "Mission Mexico. Got it."

"Angels on it." Carmy lifted his arms in the air.

***

Mark almost ran to Paige's office. Seeing her door half open he hopped sideways passed Amy and barged on in. Paige was standing at a file cabinet when Mark grabbed her around the waist, twisted her around and swung her up off her feet.

"We did it. The client loved it. We are brilliant together, darling."

Paige wrapped her arms around his neck. Holding her, he didn't even think of how it would feel until her body formed to his. Not wanting to let go of her, still he sat her on the top of her desk. Putting his arms on both sides of her, he leaned forward, their lips almost touching.

Having her trapped, he looked into her eyes. "We are going to throw a party for the whole agency. And then..." His voice went to a whisper. "...you and I are going to celebrate, just the two of us."

Paige looked over his shoulder. "We have company." Patting his shoulder she said low in his ear.

Without moving from his place he looked back over his shoulder. There stood Amy, with a look of glee on her face. Constance, in her 'hell bent for leather' stance. The design crew, waiting to know what was going on and last but not least the Partners. Mark's shouts as he bounced down the hall must have set off a chain reaction.

Paige pushed gently against his arms as she slid off the desk and brushed at her clothes. Stepping aside, he stood behind her.

"Come on in folks. We have great news."

As people filed in the small office, Mark announced with a flair of his arms. "The Ad campaign for Ben Olson was a huge success. I just got off the phone with his people."

Applause and cheers rose to the ceiling. There was lots of hugging and slapping on the back.

Rubin came up to Paige and grabbed her in a big bear hug. "Girl, we did it."

Mark slapped them both on the back. "You did." He turned to the crowd. "Amy, Brad. Get a party set up for tomorrow after work. It's Friday, so make it awesome."

The two nodded, turned and walked out to Amy's desk, talking a mile a minute.

Constance pushed Paige out of the way as she threw her arms around Mark's neck. "Mark, dear. I knew your charming ways would win them over."

Trying to disengage himself from her clutches, he saw Paige step back with a smirk on her face.

"Constance." He finally got her off him. "Paige was the artist. She knew exactly how to please Ben."

Shooting a glancing look over her shoulder in Paige's direction. "Yes, of course. Mark, I say you and I go celebrate."

"That is a great idea." He grabbed Paige's hand and drug her through all the people. Out her office door, to the elevator. Looking back, he could see all the people in the office watching them. Most were smiling, except Constance.

If looks could kill.

The bell dinged and the doors slid open. Mark still held Paige's hand, pulled her into the small square. Swinging her around they both hit the back wall.

Mark smiled to himself.

"Where are we going?" He looked over at Paige when she spoke.

"Just out. I need some fresh air. I am on such a high." He chuckled. "Actually, I am starved. How about a late lunch?"

Her smile was breath-taking. So sexy.

Her voice made him grin. "Okay. Let's eat."

"Where?" Mark looked up at the numbers as they changed.

The doors opened to the main floor.

Paige waved her arm to him. "Surprise me."

***

"Now…" Sid was flying behind the couple as they headed down the sidewalk. "…we need to get her to tell him she will be in Mexico for Christmas."

Carmy was puffing trying to keep up with Sid. "Gotch ya'."

"She and her mom will be leaving in a

week and a half." Sid was way into getting this done.

Carmy was still behind a little. "I know."

"Richard and his family have gone back to Maine."

"I know." Carmy could hardly get the words out.

"Mark and his father will be alone for Christmas."

"I know!" Carmy tried to pick up speed.

Sid stopped in mid-air. "So what's the plan?"

Huffing, Carmy stopped by Sid. "I don't know right now. Let's just see how lunch goes. We'll see an opportunity. We'll pounce on it."

Sid looked at the heavy breathing angel. "You okay?"

Carmy nodded his head. "Yes, I'm fine. But we are losing our people."

Sid snapped his head sharply as Mark and Paige disappeared into Christopher's. "Well let's go. We can't stay here gabbing when there are things to do."

Carmy followed after Sid. "I know."

***

The hostess recognized the couple from work lunches when they walked into the mostly empty restaurant. Leading them to a corner booth, the room was lit with low lights and a diffused candle on the table. The circular booth allowed them to sit across from one another, face to face.

Mark dropped his head against the back of the booth. "Man what a rush." Straightening up, he tilted his head and looked at Paige. "Aren't you just...ecstatic?"

Paige grinned.

He's so cute.

"Yes, this is going to move the agency right up to the top. Not that they weren't already, but this is huge."

Mark leaned forward, took hold of her hands. "What about you? It was your idea. Your concept."

Paige tried to ignore the sparks that were flying between them. "And my team. I can't do anything..."

"Excuse me. Would you like something to drink?"

Mark still held her hands. Without asking her or looking at the male waiter. "Champagne." His eyes bore into hers. "The best."

"Well, as I was saying my team is extraordinary."

His gray eyes were dark almost black. "How did we get you, Paige?"

"I just applied. The agency has a great reputation, so it was worth a shot." Becoming aware that he still had hold of her hands, his thumbs were stroking her palms.

"Why Wisconsin?"

"It was new. Different." His touch was arousing her senses.

"And your mom?"

The words were hard to get out. "Moved here later."

"So you were the pioneer?" His sexy little smile was charming.

"So to speak." She couldn't decide if she should remove her hands.

Would that be rude?

Or, just enjoy his touch and attention.

The waiter bringing the champagne made the decision for her. Mark released her. Putting her palms under the table, she wiped the moisture off on her napkin.

Pouring one flute, the waiter handed it to Mark. When he sipped it, nodding, the other flute was filled and handed to Paige.

Why do they assume the man knows wine better than a woman?

Dismissing the question that had no real business being there, Paige clinked glasses with Mark.

"So, what do we do now, Paige?"

"I beg your pardon?"

"Now, the big project is done, what are we going to do?"

"Well I am going to Mexico with my mother for Christmas."

"Mexico? No big lavish Christmas with tree with a big dinner and lots of family and presents?"

Paige circled the rim of her glass with her index finger, looking down at the white table cloth. "No. Mom gave all that up when she and Dad divorced."

"I'm sorry."

The compassion in his voice made her look up.

Paige shrugged. "It's okay. I'm just glad it's to a warmer climate this time. Last year was an Alaskan cruise. Ever seen a glacier fall into the ocean?

Mark chuckled. "No, can't say I have."

"Well it's not that great. It was cold and snowed all the time we were there." She smiled at remembering how she just stayed on the ship and read. "At least this year I might get out to enjoy some sun."

"You didn't like the snow? You live in Wisconsin."

"That's the point. Why would you leave cold and snow to go to cold and snow? A break should be something different."

He chuckled. "That's very logical. Are you always so logical? Ever spontaneous?"

Her defenses rose. "I can be spontaneous?"

"Really? Tell me how?"

"I...I...read the ending of a book before I finish it. There."

"Actually that's very logical. Why waste your time reading something you're not going to like the end of." He leaned forward. "Why not live for the adventure of finding out?"

"I can do adventure." She finished her drink with one gulp. "Hit me again." Slapping her glass on the table she dared him.

Empting the bottle, Mark motioned for the waiter to bring another. Three bottles later, they scooted to the center of the booth. Laughing and giggling, Paige let down her defenses and relaxed with him.

Finally he pulled her from the table and guided her out the door. The night air, cleared her head somewhat, but she leaned heavily on Mark's arm as he took her to her apartment, got her inside and onto her bed.

Covering her up with a blanket, she looked up at his beautiful eyes. "You have pretty eyes." Her words slurred.

"Good night, Paige."

She heard his voice through her champagne induced haze.

"Good night, Mark."

***

The two angels high-fived.

CHAPTER SIX

The snow storm headed for Wisconsin came down from the north leaving a trail of several feet of the white powder.

Paige and Vivian scheduled a taxi for six in the morning to be sure and get checked in for their eight o'clock flight. The twenty-third of December and the airport was crowded with holiday travelers. Pushing their way up to the ticket counter, Paige was relieved as she watched their bags travel down the conveyer belt into the small dark hole. *I hope they get to our plane.*

Fighting to get back out of the crowd, the two women were jostled and separated as they made their way to the escalators. As the steps moved with Paige, Vivian was several steps behind. Glancing back, Paige checked to make sure her mom was still there. Her glancing was misinterpreted by a young man between them as flirting and he kept winking.

Vivian's on her own getting off.

Facing forward, Paige stepped off the moving stairs and moved to the side. The winking man started to stop by Paige, but she shook her head no and he proceeded on.

The security check was long and tedious. People argued, took their sweet time doing what they were instructed to do.

Just do what you are told, idiots.

A break in the crowd let Paige shake off the confinement of being in the cattle crowd of people. Vivian was just getting through the scanner. As Paige waited, she looked around at the people traveling to all different destinations. Parents with small children, young and older couples probably going home to family. A touch on her arm from Vivian snapped her out of her day dreaming.

Vivian's words were pure gold. "Let's get a cup of coffee."

Relief flooded over Paige. All that was left was to board the plane at Gate A and go where it was warm, calm and relaxing. Nodding she walked with her mom to the coffee vendor. It was seven twenty-three.

The waiting area was packed full. Finding two separate seats, Paige and Vivian waited the last few minutes until boarding. A brief layover in Chicago, then on to Mexico. By four this afternoon she would be sipping on a Mai Tai. Two weeks was the longest vacation she had taken in two years. With the big project done, Mark insisted she take a long break. In fact she almost got the feeling he wanted her away for awhile.

Nonsense. He was just rewarding me for my hard work.

The girl on the speaker interrupted her thoughts. As the rows were announced, groups of people rose and migrated towards the boarding doors. Vivian and Paige joined up just before handing the young man their tickets. Neither spoke as they went through the long ramp to the plane doors.

Elbowed by people they took their seats and buckled in. Paige always liked take off. The flash of speed then the floating in air, gave her a rush.

Finally, on my way.

Vivian ordered a white wine, Paige a lite beer. Swallowing the cool yellow brew, small fine flakes of snow flew passed her window.

Good-bye snow, cold, ice. For the next few days I will be on the beach, in a pool, or on the veranda having a tropical drink. Maybe a fling with a hot cabana boy. Mmmmm.

Her head hit the back of her seat as she let go of work and her mundane life to think of some hot romance.

Yes, I need some short-lived passion in my life.

"So, what's the deal with you and Mark Winston?"

Vivian's voice caused her to snap sharply back to reality. "What are you talking about?"

"Well he's a nice young man. Are you interested?"

"No."

Liar, liar pants on fire.

"Not even the least little bit?" Vivian raised an eyebrow.

"Mom. Stop it. He is my boss

and the boss' son. Not going there."
Paige turned in her seat to face her
mother. "What about your love life?"

The smile that crossed her
mother's face was disturbing.

"Oh, I have some men friends."
Vivian sipped her wine.

Paige was appalled. "Some?"

"A few."

"A few?"

"Are you going to repeat every
word I say? You act upset?"

"I...I...I'm not upset. It's your life.
But honestly, a few?"

"Look. I enjoy many things and
many men doing many things." She
smirked a little. "I am a free woman, as
are you. Live a little, hon."

Paige grabbed the magazine in
her lap, flipped the pages quickly.
"Done talking about this."

The seat shook from the
vibration of Vivian's chuckle.

**

"We're going to Mexico." Carmy was
bouncing around the airplane's cabin.

Sid was on the head rest of Paige's seat.
"Mark and his father have already left in their

private jet. Does Vivian know they are coming?"

Carmy circled around the two women. "Yes, Tom told her. Thus the questions about Mark."

Sid pondered. "So was Vivian the one that requested us?"

"Her and Tom."

"Both?"

"Yes, they both want the kids to find love in the right place."

"But with each other?"

"Not exactly. It just worked out that way."

"Wow. That's sweet." Sid put his hands over his heart. "So do we play love angels to Vivian and Tom?"

"No, they aren't part of it."

"Why? I mean we are on a roll here."

Carmy blew on his fingers, rubbed them on his chest. "They don't want love, they just want to screw around."

"Angel! Just the thought."

"Well, it is the truth."

"Fine. Let's not discuss those two. We have enough to do with the other two."

"That works for me. "Cause we're going to Mexico." Carmy took a flying leap down the aisle.

***

Somehow the storm caught them at Chicago. Grounded, they sat on the runway as the ice pounded the plane. Paige squirmed wanting to get this show on the road. The ice storm let up after a few hours. The trucks de-iced the plane, again they took to the sky.

Landing in Phoenix, Paige pushed her mother to get in the flow of people and off the plane. There were less than forty-five minutes to change planes.

Their flight was delayed. Caught in a snow storm. Next plane, two hours.

Okay, get to the gate then just wait.

Breathless, Paige dragged Vivian down the walkway to the trams, moving her along like herding sheep. Passing several food kiosks, Paige was on a mission to get back on the damn plane and get going. Reaching the gate, Vivian jerked her arm from Paige.

"Okay, we are at the gate. We have thirty minutes until we board. I want a hamburger."

Paige's body slumped. So intent on getting to the plane, she did not stop to think about eating or anything else.

"You're right. Go get what you want. I'm going to the restroom and I'll meet you back here."

Juggling her hot dog, chips and bottled water, just as Paige got to the boarding area the flight attendant announced. "The flight to Mexico has been delayed because of mechanical trouble."

Vivian came up behind Paige just as an irate passenger asked the all important question. "How long?"

Keeping the calm she had been trained to keep the girl said. "You will be put on the next flight. It will depart in two hours."

Paige dumped the fast food she just bought in the trash. Vivian starred at her daughter as she took the food and drink from Vivian, threw them in the trash, also. Paige answered her questioning look. "We are going back down to one of those full serve restaurants, have a good dinner and a drink. I really need a drink."

Three hours later Paige was doubly relieved when at last they boarded the plane. Sitting down, Vivian and Paige were exhausted and there were still four more hours of flying. As the plane took off, she folded her arms.

Next stop. Sun and sand.

It was well past midnight when the bell boy unlocked their door to their room. Their bags did not arrive with them. Paige was dead on her feet. Walking straight into the first bedroom of the two bedroom suite, she dropped her purse, laptop bag and anything else on the floor. Kicked off her shoes. Plopped face down on the bed, rolling onto her back.

Vivian stood in the doorway. "You need anything?"

"Just sleep." Paige rolled in the bedspread, grabbed a pillow for her head. "Night. Mom."

***

"Now that was a rough trip. We should have flown on our own." Sid lay down on the top of the dresser.

Carmy was curling up on the

headboard. "My thoughts also."

"So is Mark here?"

"Yes, right next door."

"He arranged that?"

"Yes, he is a very resourceful guy."

Sid yawned and snuggled down. "The fun begins tomorrow."

"That it will. N-i-g-h-t." Carmy drifted off. ***

Fighting with the fluffy comforter she tangled herself up in, Paige sat up when she found a spot that would free her. Looking around, she pushed her hair out of her eyes and finally figured out where she was.

I am in Mexico.

Fighting her way out of the rest of the bedding, she lowered her bare feet to the hard, cool tile. Having no idea what time it was, she pressed the button on her phone.

Nine am. Not bad after the disastrous trip yesterday.

Not hearing anyone stirring, she peeked out the bedroom door. The other bedroom door was open. No Vivian in the bed.

No longer concerned about being

quiet she marched through the suite. The kitchenette was sparse, however there was a coffee pot. Paige made coffee then decided to take a shower.

Clothes? Did our bags ever get here?

Looking around, she didn't see any.

Great!

Talking to no one since she was alone. "I need a shower. I need clothes and I need food."

Going to the phone on the table she dialed the front desk. "Concierge, please." Tapping her fingers on the glass top.

"Good morning sir. I am in need of some clothes as I arrived last night and my bags didn't."

He transferred her to the dress salon. Giving her size and needs, she was pleased that by the time she got out of the shower there would be something for her to wear.

Hanging up, she yanked up the phone and pressed 'room service'. Ordering everything she could think of, she tromped into the bathroom. Turning on the shower, she stripped off yesterday's clothes and stepped into the hot steamy water.

Thank goodness the resort provided toiletries.

Feeling clean and rejuvenated, all she had to wear was a bathing suit. With a towel around her, she pulled it out of her carry-on bag. Padding to the coffee pot, she poured a cup and took the first gulp of the morning.

Oh, yes.

Back in the bathroom, she stepped into the new bathing suit she bought at the last minute and threw in her bag. Glad she did. Putting her arm through the soft, fluffy, white, French terry robe provided by the hotel, she didn't belt it, just let it hang.

The knock on the door told her one of her two needs had arrived. Hearing 'room service', her stomach growled low to let her know it was time to eat.

Opening the door, she stepped back to let in the boy with the cart.

"The patio, please." Catching him looking at her barely clad body that showed through the gap in the robe, she started to belt it but thought.

No, be a little darning. It's a vacation.

With Paige following, he sat the table with all her favorite breakfast foods. Signing the bill adding a good tip, she gave him a smile and watched as he left.

Food. Oh yeah. This is what I needed.

Pouring a fresh cup of coffee, she sat down, letting her robe fall open. Taking a deep breath of sea air, she took in the beautiful setting. White sands, emerald color waves, palm trees everywhere.

Filling her plate, her fork was half way to her mouth when she heard voices from the suite next door. Immediately, with her free hand she grabbed to close the robe then released it.

I don't know them. They will only be a part of my life for two weeks.

Continuing her fork to her mouth, she was savoring the delicious flavors when a man came around the edge of her patio.

Mark Winston!

Her mouth full, she spit out her

words with her food. "What are you doing here?"

Dressed in jean shorts, a white chest hugging v-neck tee shirt, un-tucked, and sandals.

God he looks good.

This time she did grab the front of her robe. Clinching it tightly in her hands, she dropped her fork letting it bounce on the glass table top.

"Don't let me interrupt your breakfast."

"What are you doing here?"

"I came with my Dad."

"Here?"

Pulling out a chair, he sat across from her. "Why not here? Do you mind me being here?"

"Well, no. It just seems like quite a coincidence."

Paige relaxed her death grip on the robe, but not enough to allow a look. She was totally mortified that Mark was here and she was as underdressed as she was.

"Fate is what makes the world go round."

"Mark, honestly. This is making me very uncomfortable."

"Who's uncomfortable?" Paige gasped as Tom Winston came into view with no one on his arm other than Vivian.

"Mom?" Paige sat back hard in the chair. She still had a death grip on her robe.

"Darling. It's great that we know some people, don't you think?"

"Yes, but how did you know we were at this resort?"

Everyone seemed to answer at once.

Vivian looked over at Tom. "I might have mentioned it."

"Viv said something about it." Tom agreed.

Mark gave her a wicked smile. "You told me."

Addressing Mark, Paige eyed him. "I did?....I did. But I didn't think you were planning on coming here."

"Well it sounded like such a good idea."

The knock at the door drew Paige's attention. "I ordered some clothes. We haven't got our bags have we?"

"Not yet, but the airline is looking

into it." Vivian smiled as Paige stood up still gripping her robe. "Are you naked under there?"

"No. I have on my bathing suit, thank you."

"Oh that cute little one you bought just before we left?" Vivian headed towards her. "Let me see."

Paige gripped the robe tighter, tying the belt tight around her waist. "No, mother." Clinching her teeth. Glancing at Mark she saw the gleam in his eyes.

His low, sexy voice washed over her. "How little?"

Turning on her heels, she went back inside and straight to the door. Pulling it open, she was greeted by a sales girl, with a name tag that said Brittney. Arms full of clothes on hangers and in bags, she carried a nice, 'let me sell you the world' smile.

Paige stepped back and motioned to the couch in the sitting area. A swirl of colors and pieces of clothes spread across the furniture.

Keeping her eyes on the business at hand, her mind was on Mark.

Where is he?"

Feeling a warm breath on her neck his words brought goose bumps to her neck.

"Be sure and keep the sun dress. It's Christmas Eve and we are dining and dancing tonight."

CHAPTER SEVEN

The resort went all out for Christmas Eve. White sparkling lights strung on every available tree and reflected in the crystal clear pools. Tables were covered in red table clothes, white gardenias and white candles as center pieces. The viewing deck over looked the shimmering sand. Palm trees lined the path to the ocean. A calm sea, the waves washed lazily up on the shore. Paige stepped out the doors of her room onto her patio. The blue and green swirl print dress, Mark suggested she keep, was a soft, flowing silk. A little more money than she should have spent. For once, at least this time, she was glad she went for the gold. The halter top dress looked good on her. Swirling around her ankles, it felt as expensive as it was. Pulling the shawl that matched around her bare shoulders, she shivered. Not knowing if it was the cool breeze or the aspects of the evening, she took a deep breath.

Vivian came up behind. Paige smiled at her mother.

Vivian patted her daughter's arm. "Try to have a good time tonight, darling."

"I am planning on it. But..." Paige never finished her sentence as Mark and Tom rounded the corner from their room.

Tom went immediately to Vivian, kissed her cheek and took her arm. His face beaming as he led her away.

Mark just stood looking at Paige, his hands in his pockets. She couldn't help but notice he looked quite good in his summer causal. At work his dress was business formal. Tonight his relaxed navy trousers and deep purple shirt accented his dark gray eyes. The tie, a beautiful blend of purples and navy, he wore only accentuated his aura of sexuality.

Twirling around, Paige laughed over her shoulder. "I should make you pay for this dress, you wanted it so bad. Cost me a fortune."

Stopping her with his arms, he

closed the gap between them. His lips were curled in a wicked grin. "I would gladly pay, to be able to see you in it."

Paige knew she was blushing. His body was hard against her. She steered clear of touching him as much as she could, but now she felt the same feelings she wanted to avoid. Her hands on his chest she could feel the muscles. The comfort that came from his arms surprised her. Tearing her gaze from his was almost impossible. It was like who was going to blink first.

"We need to go..." Paige's mind failed her.

Where the hell are we going?

"...to dinner?" He finished for her.

"Dinner. Dinner would be nice."

His smile deepened. "Can you promise me one thing, Paige?"

The way he said her name was like a warm mist, touching her skin. "What?" At this moment she was willing to agree to anything.

"Relax."

She chuckled. "That's it?"

Returning her smile. "Yes, just relax and let go. You are so always on guard."

"Being on guard keeps me out of trouble."

"Well, for the next few days, be adventurous."

"And if I get into trouble?"

"I'll be there to catch you."

Now that sounds like an offer I can't refuse.

***

"Sid, Sid?" Did you see that? The sexual tension. The vibes. Oh, wow this is going to be so easy."

"How do you figure?"

"What is to stop them from falling in love? They are almost there."

"Her convictions."

"What convictions?"

"Not to 'fish off the company pier' as she stated right up front. Not to fall in love, just fall in like…"

"Oh pooh. None of that is for real…"

"What do you mean, not real? This is how the woman thinks."

Following the couple to their table to join Tom and Vivian, Carmy was still disagreeing with Sid. "Things are going to change. Trust me."

"Isn't that what God told Noah?"

"Yes, and it turned out all right."

"All right? They almost drowned."

"Ahh. Almost, but not quite."

***

At the table the four enjoyed a holiday meal of the most elegant kind. Mark made sure Paige always had a full glass of Mai Tais. As she loosened up, she became more enjoyable and funny. Vivian swapped stories with Paige about her childhood, Mark treasured the history of her life lessons he was getting. Her laugh was real and caused him to chuckle as she recalled situations with gestures. Her hands would wander over to his arm or his shoulder as she gave details. Putting his arm on the back of her chair, he could feel the heat from her bare skin through his sleeve. When she curled into his side with laughter, he held her for just a moment. As the drinks took effect, she would lay her head on his shoulder.

A salsa band started playing around midnight. At that point, Mark stood up and reached out his hand for her. Tipsy, she smiled the sexist smile and sensually placed her hand into his, letting him wind their way to the dance floor. With a sigh, she settled into his arms, her cheek against his. Her hips gyrated with his in rhythm to the music. The delicate aroma of a fresh, light flowery scent drifted up. Aware of the silkiness of her skin as his hand traveled down her bare back, he could feel the goose bumps rise.

Still her body moved with him. Her hair felt like smooth velvet on his cheek. The night magic only heightened his desire for her. She had smitten him with her first angry words. Her first defiant remark. Even her 'down to business' stance turned him on.

For weeks he was kept at a distance by her. Tonight he was holding this feisty, beauty of a woman.

Go slow my man. Don't scare her off.

When the song ended she stayed in his arms. So he held her as they swayed to the second song. At the third, he ask.

"Are you awake?"

Her chest heaved with a deep breath. "Yes, why?"

"You aren't fighting with me."

"Yeah, well enjoy it while you can." Her face turned to him. Taking his lips into hers, she captured his mouth in a kiss that made his head reel.

Growling low he returned her kiss with his entire body, surrounding her as they danced, crushing his mouth to hers. Starving, he dived deeper into her mouth.

She moaned a rich animal like sound.

Against his will, he pulled back. His eyes intensely searched hers. Tilting her head, he could see she was questioning his action. Gently cupping her chin he spoke low and certain.

"Don't make promises you can't keep." ***

Why was 'the kiss' all I am remembering from last night?

Paige sat up slowly, but to her amazement there was no fuzzy head. No headache. No side effects to drinking last night.

And why is that?

Because dear girl, you weren't drunk.

But I kissed Mark.

And enjoyed ever minute of it.

Shit! I did.

Enough of this talking to one's self. Leaving the bed, she went into the bathroom, then the shower. As the water beat on her back, she thought about how good he felt when they danced. How much she wanted to see him again. She would. Today. Somewhere in the back of her mind she recalled agreeing to go wave running.

Whatever the hell that is? The waves in Wisconsin are far and few.

Well, surely it required a bathing suit. And a pair of jean shorts and a tank. Water shoes. She picked up the brochure laying on the nightstand. Skimming over it, she thought of all the activities offered. Having Mark to do them with would be fun.

Walking out to the living area, she glanced up to see Tom, Vivian and Mark on the veranda having breakfast. Since this was a happy morning, she let the smile she felt on the inside, glow on her face.

As soon as Mark saw her, a grin broke across his face as he stood up. The empty chair next to him had her name written all over it. Passing her mother, she bent down and kissed her cheek.

"Morning, mother." Straightening up she nodded to Tom. "Mr. Winston. Good morning."

"Tom. Call me Tom we're on vacation."

Calling him by his first name would feel very strange but, it was only appropriate under the circumstances.

Mark pulled her chair out. "Ms. Paige. You are absolutely beaming this morning."

"Mr. Winston. I slept like a log. That is if logs sleep."

"And you are no worse for the wear from last night?"

Sitting down, Paige took her napkin and placed it over her knees. Smiling at her Mom and Tom, she winked at Vivian. "No, last night was good for me. Made me let go of some of my uptight anxieties." Taking her first and always the best sip of coffee, she turned to Mark. "You?"

The impishness was there in his eyes. "I am...really good."

Winking at him. "Good. Now today we are wave running, right?"

Mark shrugged. "You remember that?"

"Oh, I remember everything about last night." Turning away she sat her cup down. "Everything. Mom. Tom are you going to join us?"

Laughing at the same time, they both shook their heads.

Vivian patted Tom's hand. "We are taking a tour of the shops. Tom collects Aztec art."

"We'll meet you for dinner." Tom piped in. "If you don't break a leg."

Mark rested his arm on the back of Paige's chair. "Good." Poking her with his other finger, he leaned up to her. "So eat breakfast and we will ride those mighty waves." The last word spoken on the back of her neck.

***

Sid sat up. "We are doing what today?"

"Nothing." Carmy chuckled. "They are riding wave runners. We are sitting on the dock making sure they don't kill themselves."

"Oh good. I'm just not sure about this wave thing."

"You've never been assigned to any of the coasts?" Carmy splashed his legs in the water.

"Not really. And water's not really my thing."

"Why not?"

Sid said simply. "Had a bad experience."

"On what? A cruise ship? A barge? I know a pirate ship."

"No to all of the above."

Carmy was baffled. "What then? Tell me."

"It was a small fishing craft."

"How small?"

"What difference does it make? I almost lost my person and I was in the water for hours before help arrived. There." Sid kicked the water hard.

Carmy frowned. "Okay, but you know our kind can't drown."

"No, at the time I did not know that. They failed to tell me that little bit of information."

The wave runners were like jet skis. They had those in Wisconsin. Paige even rode on them.

Piece of cake.

A young, nice looking guy was available to help. As Paige wrestled with her life jacket Carlos, as he was called, came over and helped. Mark was busy with his own, until he looked up and saw Paige and Carlos. Paige watched as he stopped what he was doing and came over to them.

Paige was standing with her feet apart, arms spread eagle. Carlos was reaching between her legs to grab the belt. Snapping it into place at her crotch, he then proceeded to snap the straps across her chest. Mark's eyes were getting narrower by the minute.

Finished, Carlos bowed to Paige. "You are all tucked in nice and tight." He patted the front of the vest.

"Okay." Mark pushed him aside, stood between them, his back to Paige. "She's fine."

Paige rested her chin on Mark's shoulder. "Are you all buckled up?"

Mark started working on his

belts. "Almost. Tough little devils to fasten."

"If you need help, I can call Carlos back over here."

With a loud snap, Mark finished his last hook. "Get on the runner." He took her arm and led her to where the machines were docked. Holding her elbow he waited until she was securely on.

Carlos appeared at Mark's side. "You good, Miss?"

Mark turned to face the young man, blocking the way to Paige. "She's fine."

Carlos moved on down the line of people and machines. Mark swung his leg over the seat of his runner, turned back to look at Paige. "Ready for this?"

"You're on cowboy." With that she gunned the motor and left him in a spray of water.

For hours, they raced back and forth. Passed the breakers, the water was smoother. Through the mist of the wakes she saw him smiling, then get very intense as he barreled across the water. So engrossed in their activities Paige failed to notice the dark clouds building around them.

Mark brought his runner dead in the water. Sitting sideways in front of her, she slowed as she watched his gaze go over her head. Cutting the engine on her machine, she coasted up to him.

"What's wrong?"

"We're in trouble, darling."

Paige looked over her shoulder and gasped at the fast moving ocean storm headed for them. "What are we going to do?"

Already the ocean started to swell, pitching them up and down. Mark looked around. Paige followed his lead, searching for any kind of land.

Barely able to hear him, he shouted at her. "Over there. Go as fast as you can."

Without a pause, Paige floored the throttle and headed towards the small line of trees that could barely be seen. The wind at her back, it tossed waves along side of her. Dragging her forward, the pull of the current helped her speed. Closer and closer the sandy beach appeared. When her runner hit the bottom it stopped. Jumping off, she pulled it onto the beach. A strong wind whipped around her, rain pelted her skin like needles.

Mark?

His machine roared up beside her. Fighting the wind, he hugged her as he looked around at the land area. To the left was a large rock formation that jetted out into the water.

"Come on."

Together they fought against the harsh wind to the rock. When she could see the cave, she felt relief. Once in the cave Paige leaned against the smooth walls. Mark stood in front of her, his look intent and beckoning.

The storm outside rocked the floor of the cave, vibrating up her already over aroused body. Without either speaking they came together in a kiss, burning and demanding. His rock hard body pressed against her, sending a sizzling blaze of desire down to her sweet place.

Lightning flashed and radiated the darkness, as the thunder gave a powerful vibe. Her body was on fire, hot and ready. Together they removed each other's shirt in a rush of passion.

Throwing them aside, his hands unsnapped her jeans, pushing them and her swimming suit bottoms off.

The coolness of the air only made her want to feel the heat of him inside of her. His hands untied the suit top, freeing her breasts. His mouth took them in, lifting her off her feet. Working her hands down to his swimming trunks, she could feel his hardness.

This only heightened her need for him. Roughly pushing them down, she jumped up and wrapped her legs around his hips. His hands cupped her butt as he positioned her. Shoving her to the wall, her heels dug into the small of his back as he lifted her on to him.

She shuddered as she felt all the pinned up desire explode in her loins. Grabbing him she buried her face in his neck. Her climax spiraled up with such power she could not stop the scream as it built in her throat.

His body shuttered as he climaxed with her. The quick hot sex was overpowering yet satisfying. For several minutes she clung to him as her body and spirit recovered from the ecstasy of his love-making. Removing himself, he kissed her as they both slid down the wall to the cool wet sand.

Exhausted from the intense emotional roller coaster of outrunning the storm and allowing sexual desire to equal the raging tempest, they both collapsed to the cave floor on their backs.

Mark crawled over to the rock wall, sat with his back against it. His legs up, resting his arms on his knees, he was taking deep breaths.

Paige crawled over to him, nestled between his legs. He wrapped his arms around her.

"You okay." His voice came in gasps.

Paige couldn't speak, so she nodded.

Squeezing her, his arms gave her courage. She didn't fight the comfort she felt. As the storm continued, they watched it together. The trees bent to the ground, the wet sand swirled up and around. The forceful wave looked as tall as a house, crashing down with a power only nature could produce.

Paige shivered. Mark tightened his hold.

His voice was low and sure. "We'll be okay in here."

Leaning her head against his chest, she believed him.

***

"What do you mean you lost them? Angels don't lose people." Sid's wings flapped swiftly against his body as he hovered over Carmy.

Carmy defended himself. "I didn't lose them."

"Then where are they?"

"They're safe."

"Where?"

"In a cave on a beach a little south of here."

"And why, pray tell, are they there and we're not?"

"Because according to the plan, they needed some time together without divine intervention."

"To do what? Drown together?"

Carmy was getting a little tired of the questions. "They didn't drown. They will be back in a couple of hours."

"Why so long? What are they going to do during that time?"

Carmy chuckled. "I think they have that covered."

CHAPTER EIGHT

Paige snuggled into Mark's body. The raging storm seemed to intensify. Mark kissed the top of her head, drew her into his chest. He wanted some alone time, but being stranded in a cave was a little much.

"Well, I guess this is the answer to my hope of getting you alone." He kept his voice light.

"Wouldn't it have been easier to just ask me?" Her nervous chuckle vibrated against him.

Feeling her tremble, he wanted to comfort her. They were okay. Tropical storms have a habit of passing quickly. He turned his head and looked out the cave's opening. The two wave runners were on the beach. Being whipped ruthlessly by the rain and wind, they still stood where they were left.

His hands rubbed her arms, feeling her shiver.

"Are you cold?" Their clothes were soaked. There was nothing to warm her up but his body heat.

"Not much. So why did you want to get me alone?"

The change of subject he took as a distraction. "I came down here because I wanted to see if there could be an 'us'?"

"I thought we covered that back in Wisconsin."

"No, you covered it. Something about fishing and…"

"Off the company pier." Her voice carried a giggle. Turning in his embrace, she wiped the water from his cheek. "I never wanted to date a co-worker. It just makes problems."

"If I agree that it won't cause problems will you give a try? Just with me? I don't want you dating every man in the agency."

Paige searched his face. "Okay, I will give it a try."

His hand took hold of hers as it touched his face. The other hand drew her into him. Beginning a light teasing kiss, just enough to still her tentativeness.

When she did not pull away, he deepened his kiss. Facing him now, she was on her knees. Her arms went up around his neck.

Her eyes sparkled at him. "So you thought taking me right here in the sand was a way to convince me?"

Kissing her quickly. "It wasn't part of the plan. But it was fantastic."

"I see." A wicked gleam lit her blue eyes. "Do you think you're ready for this?"

"The question is are you?" Loving the wordplay, he was lost in her eyes.

"Oh, I have been ready for a while."

Grabbing her upper arms with both his hands, he sat her back on her ass in the sand. Still keeping his grip. "You what?"

"I've been wanting to do this quite some time now." Pushing up to a sitting position, she pulled him to her.

Inches from her face, his expression was shadowed with suspicion. "You could of told me."

"Now what fun would that be?" Her mockery made him laugh. That having this woman, after nights of painful dreams was finally a reality. Knowing he had met his match, his desire for her escalated.

Sitting crossed legged, his hold brought her close to him. "God woman. You are amazing."

Speaking against his lips. "I am surprised you could handle it."

His deep belly laugh rocked them both. "Why did you decide to have sex with me?"

"Seemed like a good idea at the time." Her words spoken against his lips.

"And now?" His tone low and sexy.

The faintest trace of humor lit her eyes. "It was a good idea."

"Just a good idea?"

"You want a medal?"

"No, I want you to tell me this is the start of something."

The silence was deafening. Finally she spoke. Her look was firm and straight. "I guess."

Mark looked down at her. "You guess? What is there to guess?"

"I can't deny I have feelings for you. Being here in Mexico caused me to let down my guard." She took his face in her hands, with fingertips brushed his wet hair away from his forehead. "I guess I hope that what happens here will work when we get back to our real world."

The tenderness of her words and her touch melted his resolve. "It will, I prom..."

Her finger on his mouth stopped his words. "Don't make promises you can't keep." Her eyes shot him a quick, sharp, simple look.

"Okay, we do this one day at a time." He sealed the deal with a kiss.

The storm passed over them. A fine mist rose from the ground as the heat and humidity returned. Paige drew back, a frown crossed her face. "One more thing. Can we not tell my mom just yet?"

"How are we going to keep it a secret?"

"I don't know. But if she knows, she will be hiring the caterer for our wedding."

Getting to his feet, he hauled her up, bringing their naked bodies together. Kissing her, he patted her butt. "Let's get dressed. Get back to the resort, before they send out the search team."

Sorting through their clothes, he tossed her swim suit top and shorts in her direction. Paige threw his trunks at him. Slipping on the pants, he grabbed his shirt. Leaving the cave, he lowered the cold wet material over his shoulders.

The wave runners were still where they were left. Paige's was on its side. Going to his, mounting it, he tried to start it. It sputtered then took hold. Hers was covered with a least a foot of sand, looked like a truck dumped a load on it.

Good. At least they had one.

Paige walked over to him, hugged his neck. He nodded to the downed runner. "Ride with me. We'll send someone back for yours."

Throwing her leg over the back seat space, she hugged his waist. "Take me home, fearless leader."

His laugh was lost on the wind, as they took off and skimmed over the now quiet sea. ***

Sid was pacing on the dock at three in

the afternoon when Paige and Mark returned to the resort.

"There they are!" Carmy jumped and shouted. The two angels on the dock had been waiting for hours.

Sid stopped, raised his head as the one wave runner came into view. "About time."

Mark coasted up to Carlos standing on the boardwalk. "Sorry, dude. Got caught in the storm. Had to take cover on a beach."

Carlos extended his hand to Paige, helped her get her footing. Mark dismounted and took her hand. They looked a sight. Like they had been windblown and tossed about. Mark explained where they left the other runner. Carlos knew exactly where he was talking about and agreed to go get the other runner.

Mark and Paige walked up the walkway together, holding hands.

Carmy pulled an invisible level in the air. "Yes."

Sid fluttered around the couple. "Something's different."

Carmy followed him. "Of course. They are now in love, duh."

A frown creased Sid's forehead. He floated in the air, flying backwards. "So our work is done? I don't have the feeling this assignment is complete."

"It's not. This is just the beginning of the relationship. We have to see this through to the wedding."

"They are going to get married?"

"Well that's the plan."

"Still something is different. Like they..."Sid snapped around to face Carmy. "They didn't?"

Carmy chuckled. "Of course they did. What century are you in?"

Sid huffed. "Know-it-all."

***

At the rooms, Mark pulled Paige towards his. "Come with me."

"I need a shower." She tried to pull back.

"I have a shower." He gathered her to him. "A nice big shower."

"Clothes?"

"You don't need them." He was walking her to the door with him.

At the sliders, he used one hand to open the door. His mouth was on her lips, her neck, her ears.

That did it. Once inside she threw her arms around his neck. He carried her to his bathroom. Kissing her again, he put her down while he removed first her clothes then his. Reaching in, he turned on the two jet shower. Their clothes lay in a scatter of sand all over the floor.

Paige went in first, the delicate spray felt refreshing as it removed the sand and salt from her skin. Mark took a wash cloth and soaped it. His hand moved over her shoulders, her back. Turning her around, her rubbed her breasts, her mid-drift, on down.

Paige stood under the shower head and let it soak her head. As Mark washed her body, she allowed the flickers of desire to lick at her. His hands touched the good places on her body. Having felt how pleasant it was to make love to him, she relished the feelings of enjoyment.

Coming up, his body scrapped hers. Touching her wet hair, he reached behind her, bringing around the shampoo. Pouring some in her hand, he watched as she lifted her arms to soap her hair, making her breasts pull upwards.

Paige moved her soap filled hand to his hair. Lathering, she pressed her body to his. Slow and seductive she massaged his head, down his neck, along his back, over his tight butt. Around to the front, she passed over his crotch, up the six pack abs, to the hair on his chest. His eyes conveyed his amusement at her touch.

Pushing her back under the second jet, the strong flow drenched them as the soap, cascaded down their bodies rinsing them clean. As the water poured over them, he kissed her deep and fervently.

"This is how we should start and end every day." He spoke as the water washed over them.

Paige took in a mouth full of water as she replied. "Making plans?"

He jerked back. "Can I?"

God she loved messing with him.

"Some, but let's do some spontaneous."

"Like what?"

"Like you feed me." She pushed him away, stepped out of the shower.

Grabbing his hotel robe, she wrapped it around her body.

As he stood in the bathroom, wrapping a towel around his waist, she threw back over her shoulder as she left. "I am ordering room service and you are paying for it. It's your fault I am so famished."

Joining her in his bedroom, he plopped down on the bed, laid back. "I can live with that. Order me some too."

Waiting for someone to answer, she spoke to him. "Oh, I plan to. You are going to need your strength if you plan on keeping me happy."

His body quivered as he hooted a deep throaty laugh. "Is that a threat or a promise?"

Someone came on the phone just as she started to quip back. Winking at him, she picked up the menu. "Yes, we need room service."

The food arrived quickly. Mark answered the door still in his towel, stopped the waiter from entering with a big tip and rolled the cart into his room. Shutting and locking his door, he stopped moving to look at Paige. She crawled in the middle of his bed, sitting cross-legged.

Taking the silver lids off of the food, he handed her plates and finally she laughed. "Stop." Handing two plates back. "I need to do just one at a time."

Replacing her food, he grabbed one and crawled up in front of her, also cross legged.

"So you want to make this into something?" Mark asked her.

Paige put one of her grapes in his mouth. He sucked her fingers in, teasing them with his tongue.

Removing her fingers, she picked up a piece of meat from his plate. Putting the food into her mouth and running her tongue around it, she watched him squirm.

"I have wanted it to be something since you dumped your coffee all over my new coat." She watched his eyes light up as she spoke her words.

"Seeing you made me lose my focus."

"You barreled into me." She threw a French fry at him.

"It was a new coat? Sorry about that. I did get it cleaned for you."

"Well, I soaked your rather pricey shoes."

Filling his mouth with food, he shook his head. "No, I deserved that. I was so nervous..."

"...and I made it worse."

"No..." taking a drink of his water. "...you made it better."

"How so?"

His eyes mirrored his feelings. "I knew if I could see those blue eyes every day I could do this."

Paige recalled her heart melting that first day. But she kept a tight hold on it until now.

Now what? Now I will see where it goes.

Feeling full, Paige picked up her plate, untangling herself from the bed, placed her leftovers on the full cart.

Never had she felt so content and so exhausted at the same time. Mark got up behind her.

"I need a nap. I'm going to my room. I'll return your robe later."

His smile told her this was not how it was going to be. "No, sleep here. With me." In one swoop he pulled the covers back, took her hand

and guided her into the bed.

Crawling in with her, he wrapped his arms around her. The feel of his body was so comforting, she let sleep engulf her.

***

Tom held Vivian's hand as she stepped down from the hotel's shuttle bus. They had stayed several hours longer in the city than planned. Since their plan was to meet up with Mark and Paige for dinner, Mark tried to call them, but it went straight to voice mail.

It was well past ten o'clock when they finally reached their room. Hands full of packages, they stopped at her door first. Vivian turned to Tom.

"I would love to spend the night with you, but with Paige in the same suite..." She grimaced. "...it might not be a good idea."

Tom took her in his arms. "Does she know about us?"

"Not really. She's a little uptight in that area. Your sons?"

Placing her hands on his chest, she ran them over his toned upper body. For his age Tom Winston was in great shape.

"Not really. They both think I have a dull social life."

His light chuckle caused her to chuckle also. "Well I am hoping this trip gets her in the swing for fun."

His body conformed to hers. "Well I think my son might get her to loosen up a bit. He is so smitten with her."

Vivian couldn't hide her enthusiasm. "I hope so. She needs a little ump in her life."

His eyes sparkled. "How about you spend the night with me?"

"Your son..."

"...sleeps like a bear. Your daughter?"

"Likes to sleep late. I can be back in our suite before she orders coffee."

Vivian was liking this idea. Her body was heating up with the thoughts of having the whole night with Tom. "Let me put these bags inside."

Slipping her card key in the slot, the door opened quietly. Soundlessly they put the bags just inside the door. Vivian glanced at her daughter's room and saw that the door was shut.

Sleep tight dear Paige.

Backing out, Vivian took Tom's arm. "She's out for the night. They must have used all their energy today doing that wave thing."

Only a few feet from Vivian's door, Tom quietly unlocked his room. As they tiptoed in Mark's door was closed. Without any sound, Tom led her to his room. The door was ajar. Pushing slowly, it opened without a squeak. They slithered in, Tom push the door shut holding the knob so there would be no click.

Giggling like school children, they came together. Vivian put her fingers to her lips. "S-h-h-h."

Tom kissed her then began unbuttoning her blouse. "They will never know."

***

Sid and Carmy sat outside the two rooms in a palm tree. Deep in thought, Sid spoke first.

"I don't have a good feeling about this. They are going to run into each other tomorrow morning."

"Maybe not." The ever optimistic Carmy frowned.

"You're not sure."

"Yes I am."

"No you're not."

"Okay, not one hundred percent sure."

Sid glared at the always 'happy' little angel. "What is going to happen if Mom finds out daughter is sleeping with the son and vice versa?"

"Well Mom will be ecstatic. Daughter will be devastated."

"So this is not a totally good thing?"

Carmy made a face. "Not totally."

Wringing his hands, Sid looked towards the windows where Paige was sleeping. "Is this going to screw up our plans?"

"Don't know. We have to see how this plays out."

The scowl on Sid's face told it all. "So what is our part in this?"

"Get Paige out of there before she sees Mom."

With a shrug of his shoulders, Sid nestled down in the branch. "Not a big deal." Murmuring he continued. "No, not at all. Easy as pie. Walk in the park."

CHAPTER NINE

The feeling of male arms on her body, bewildered Paige at first. Stretching her legs, she rubbed her feet along the calves of her bed companion. The events of the day before came back in a faint rush of delightful memories.

Mark.

Lifting her arms over her head, she felt him budge.

His raspy voice vibrated against her neck. "What time is it?"

"I have no idea." Realigning her body she reached over him to get her phone. Glancing out the window, the day was just dawning.

So early morning.

Leaning her breasts on his chest, she was aware of his hands stroking her butt.

How good does that feel!

The read-out on the phone said five a.m. "Good, I can get to my room before Mom knows I wasn't there all night." Lying back down on the bed, she ran her hand through his hair.

His lips came to her demanding. "We'll meet at breakfast and pretend nothing happened?"

Speaking against his lips. "We can do this." Pushing him off the bed, he caught himself before he hit the floor with a thud.

Paige stepped over him as she got out of bed. Still in his robe, she stood for a moment looking around the room. The room service cart was piled high with half eaten food and dirty dishes. A memory of waking up and eating in the night, then back to snuggling with Mark, sent a chill down her body. Walking into the bathroom, she looked down at the pile of dirty clothes on the floor.

I can't wear them to go back to my room.

Daintily she lifted the grungy swim suit, shorts and shirt, carried them back to where Mark stood, naked and so appealing. His towel must have fallen off while they slept as it was tangled with the sheets.

His look was inviting, but she needed to keep her mind on the task at hand.

"I need to go." Departing hastily was the best choice right now.

His voice echoed behind her. "Wait. Let me get some pants."

Turning to wait, she noticed how smoothly the clean pair of jean shorts glided over his ass.

Joining her at the door, he reached around and unlocked the sliders and pulled back the curtains. His hand on her back, he guided her outside to her set of sliding doors. As she unlocked the doors, he licked and sucked on the back of her neck.

Once the door was open she turned in his arms. "See you at breakfast?"

"Most certainly." His kiss assured her she would be in his arms and making sweet love to him at some point that day.

Taking off his robe, she handed it to him on the end of her finger. His eyes lingered over her body a split second before he took it.

As they parted, she looked around her room. Too neat. Messing up her bed, she threw the dirty clothes in a corner of the bathroom. Turning on the shower, she already missed the feel of his hands as she put her head under the running water.

***

Vivian woke up too early to stay up, but she was thirsty. Not familiar with what was in Tom's kitchen, she wanted something other than water, so she was going to chance it.

A night light gave out enough glow, she could see where she was going, so she didn't run into things. In the fridge was orange juice, she poured a glass, was carrying it back to the room when she heard Mark's door open. Hurriedly she slipped through Tom's bedroom door, but kept it cracked to observe what was going on. Mark was wheeling an overloaded cart of room service towards the front door.

Vivian thought that was odd. There was way too much food for one person.

That's it. There was more than

one person in his room! Paige?

Mark was moving quietly and slowly, trying real hard not to make noise. After he got the cart out in the hallway, his step was light and bouncy as he went back to his room.

"That's a boy that just got laid." Tom's low voice made her jump.

She turned and smacked him on the arm. "You scared me." Stopping with her hand on his, he closed the door behind her. "Do you really think so? Paige?"

"I would think so. Who else?"

"You mean while we were...?" Pointing her thumb towards the door. "...they were." The irony of the situation boiled inside of her. Burying her face in Tom's chest, her body shook with laughter.

Tom's body joined hers in the hilarity of the situation. "Well, what do you know."

Vivian headed for the bathroom. Tossing her words back at Tom, "I know I need to get to my room, or my daughter will die of embarrassment if she ever realizes that I was here when she was.

Helping her wrap enough clothes around her to get down the hall, Tom watched from his door. Waving to him she slipped into her room.

Once inside, she treaded lightly to her bedroom. Paige's door was shut, but Vivian heard the shower running. Getting in her room without detection, she leaned against her closed door and sighed.

Looking at her made bed, she slipped out of her clothes and climbed in.

I need a couple of hours of sleep.

***

"Whew." Sid breathed a sigh of relief.

The two angels were still in the tree, watching the characters as they moved around to their different destinations.

Carmy leaned back. "See I told you Mom would be glad. Daughter needs to stay clueless."

"So what are their plans today?" Sid didn't know if he was ready for all the escapades the two assignments were capable of doing.

"For the next week they will spend time together. Build a bond and create memories."

"And what do we do?"

Carmy fluttered down to the sand. Sid joined him. "Take a break. We are on hiatus."

Sid shuffled behind Carmy. "For how long."

"Until they need us. And they will."

***

The day was one of those gorgeous tropical days well worth its money. Seventy perfect degrees, the ocean sparkled a bright emerald green against the off white sands. By nine a.m. the beach was filling with people.

Mark was first at the table. On the veranda outside his suite, he was anxious to see Paige. Even though he had been anxious every day to see her since they had met, today was different. Today he could touch her, feel her, visualize her naked and have an accurate picture.

Delighted to see that the next person to arrive was Paige. They both glanced around then embraced for a long, slow, tantalizing kiss. Mark's hands caressed her with slow sensual stokes. Her body responded and aroused his desire.

He groaned in her ear. "Let's spend the day in bed."

She buried her face in his neck. "We can't here. But I promise when we get home we will.

Laughing, he smacked her butt affectionately. "Don't make promises you can't keep."

"I'm not." Her words told him it was in his future.

I can live with that.

"I am starved." Tom's voice broke them apart. Each grabbed their chair, scraping them on the flagstone floor in unison. Tom pushed back the screen on the sliders, walked out and stretched. "Beautiful morning, don't you think?"

"I totally agree." Vivian's chirpy little voice sounded as she walked around the corner.

Tom pulled out the chair for Vivian, gave her a peck on the cheek as she sat down.

Shaking out his napkin, Tom spoke to the group in general. "So what are the plans for today?"

"Horseback riding." Paige picked

up her juice glass, reaching for the pitcher.

Mark picked up the pitcher and poured her some orange juice. "Zip lines."

Paige turned to look at him. "Zip lines? What the hell is that?"

He put his arms out in front of him. "It's like flying through the trees. Like Peter Pan."

"You're kidding?" Narrowing her eyes.

Tom cut in. "So how did the wave..."

Mark turned away from Paige. "...running. We got caught in a storm. Had to ditch the machines and hold up in a cave." He caught the look that passed between Tom and Vivian.

They know.

He glanced at Paige. Busy buttering her bread, she missed it.

Vivian put down her fork. "Oh, my. Are you alright?"

"Yes, mother." Paige looked up. "We're fine. We found a cave to hold up in until the storm passed."

Mark didn't miss the gleam in Vivian's eyes as she questioned Paige.

"So that's why you were in bed so early?"

Paige stuttered, grabbed Mark's hand under the table. "A..a..yeah. Tried, exhausted. It was frightening."

Tom piped in. "I tried to call your cell phone. It went straight to voice mail."

Paige kicked Mark under the table. Clamping his lips so he wouldn't yell, he spoke through clinched teeth. "Turned it off. Like Paige said. Tired, exhausted, beat."

The death grip Paige had on his hand was cutting off his circulation. "So what are you two up to today?" She let up on his hand a little.

"A lunch and jazz cruise around the coast." Tom eyed his son.

Mark caught his father's look of 'I know what you're up to'. "Good. Try to meet for dinner?"

"Sure. Here at sunset." Mark nodded.

Paige released his hand before they stood up together. He shook it to get the feeling back.

"Well folks, see you later." Mark said as he and Paige separated going to their own rooms.

Vivian and Tom held it as long as they could. After a few minutes, they put their heads together, giggled.

"They're doing it aren't they?" Vivian's tone told of her delight.

Tom snickered. "Yep. They are."

***

New Year's Eve was their last night together in Mexico. The festivities started late, ten o'clock. It was a formal affair. Women in bright colored formals, men in black tux.

The week was spent with Mark and Paige doing all sort of physical activities during the day and sneaking around to have wild monkey sex whenever they could, day or night.

Paige had picked a dress for the night in Wisconsin. A simple taupe chiffon that looked nice, and very practical. Not in a particular practical mood, she ventured down to the dress shop and found a hot, sizzling red dress. Form fitting it was the most daring dress she had ever considered. Complete with red rhinestone heels, she felt like "the lady in red". Spending the day at the spa, she told Mark to leave her alone and go occupy himself.

She did it all. Massage, waxing, nails and toes. Make-up and hair, all she had left to do was slip that totally sexual dress over her head and go.

Vivian met her in the living area in a spectacular black gown. Her eyes widened as Paige exited her bedroom, ready to go.

"Wow." Vivian took in the whole look. "You look fantastic. My little girl has grown up." Faking weeping, Paige laughed with her mother.

"Okay?" Paige needed approval. She never stepped out of her box this much before.

"More than okay. You should get lucky tonight."

"Mom! Stop it." Paige said light-heartily.

Vivian linked her arm through Paige's. "Ok, the Therriault women are going to knock 'em dead tonight."

***

Tom offered to help Mark with his tie. Mark was a nervous wreck, so he took him up on the offer.

"Hold still. What is wrong with you? You are acting like this is your first date." Tom's tone carried a flippant edge.

Letting out a sigh, Mark tried to stand still long enough to get the tie straight.

Patting Mark's shoulders, Tom tilted his head and looked at his youngest son. "There."

"Thanks, Dad." Mark took a sober look at Tom. "Sorry I'm so nervous."

"Why are you?"

"I...I just want to make this a special night for Paige."

"Why so? Are you going to ask her to marry you?"

Mark chuckled. "I wish. No, I just want this thing with her to continue after we get back."

Tom sat down on the couch. "Why wouldn't it?"

Mark sat next to him. "She has this thing about co-workers dating."

"You know why don't, you?"

"No, I really don't."

Tom looked down at his hands. "Vivian's husband left her for a co-worker."

Flopping back. "Shit. I didn't

know that."

"Look son. Paige is cautious. She doesn't want to get hurt."

"Oh, Dad. I would never hurt her. I really love her." Mark chuckled.

"Then it will work out if you want it that bad." Tom stood up. "Let's go get these lovely women waiting for us."

"Right on, daddy-o"

Tom frowned. "Daddy-o?"

***

The resort's New Year Eve Party was as grand as their Christmas Eve's. A formal affair, the color scheme was black, white, gold and silver. Soft romantic music waffled up into the warm, night air. Tables covered in black tablecloths, white roses accented with gold and silver spikes as the center pieces. Luminaries reflected around the pool and down the beach walkways. A million stars sparkled in the clear sky.

Paige wanted to make a grand entrance. Vivian asked the men to meet them at the table in the dining area. As Paige leisurely walked across the courtyard towards Mark, she waited for him to notice her. He was dressed in a black tuxedo, looking more handsome as ever. Conversations stopped as she passed small groups of people. Tom's back was to her, but she was well in Mark's view.

Savoring the moment, his eyes stared at her with smoldering intensity when he looked up and saw her. Standing up, he twisted his napkin in his hand. Tom turned around and gave her an approving smile. He too rose, placed his napkin on the table by his plate. Strolling with ease to her chair by Mark, she stood waiting.

"Damn woman, you are beautiful." His words came in short, gasping breaths.

Paige cocked her head to one side. "You like?"

"Oh, yeah." His gaze followed the lines of her body in the dress. Looking back up, his eyes shone with approval. Realizing he was lacking his manners, he pulled the chair out for her. As she lowered her body to sit, Mark plopped down in his. "Marry me?"

Paige laughed as she saw the smile on his face. "No."

"Then dance with me." He held

out his hand.

Taking his out-stretched hand. "Okay."

Together they stood; she let him lead her to the dance floor. Taking her in his arms, he whispered against her hair. "This is how we started the week."

"I remember." Burying her face in his neck, she inhaled his scent of musk.

"And now?" His words were spoken against her hair.

Paige sighed. "The week is over."

As his voice carried the question, his body tensed. "And us?"

"We've only just begun." Feeling him relax, he stopped moving.

Pulling back from her. "Let's walk."

Down to the beach, her hand felt right in his hand. When they were down far enough that the music was faint, he backed her up against a palm tree.

"Don't play with me, Paige."

She watched as his eyes darkened. She wanted him to realize she was sincere. He opened up her desires, passion and heart. "I'm not."

Placing her hand aside his cheek.

"I am ready for this. We have to see how it works back home, but I want to give it a chance."

Nothing could have prepared her for the staggering intensity of his kiss. Running her fingers through the strands of his hair, she returned the strong feelings he stirred in her.

Lifting his mouth from hers. "We will work it out. I love you, Paige. I honestly do."

"I know. I am falling in love with you more every day. I'm still concerned about working together..."

"...don't be. We are strong enough to do this." His tone of determination persuaded her.

Rolling her lips, she sucked on the bottom one. "Okay."

Getting back to the table, they enjoyed a lavish dinner with their parents. Just before twelve, when the band struck the cords of Auld Lang Syne, Mark's lips were on hers as the clock struck midnight.

Grabbing two glasses of champagne, he handed one to her. They clinked and drank to the New Year. Turning to their respective parents, they clinked all four glasses.

"Happy New Year." The four chorused together.

***

"Happy New Year, Sid."

"Happy New Year, Carmy."

The two angels swayed back and forth on the metal bar separating the eating area from the beach.

"What a great year this will be." Carmy's optimistic out-look didn't rake on Sid so much tonight.

Fireworks shot up in the air, spattering the night sky with multi-colored sparkles that reflected across the ocean. The angels watched with amazement.

"It never ceases to flabbergast me how fireworks just make you all giddy inside." Carmy bounced on his butt.

Sid even had to laugh at the fireworks. They did make him feel like celebrating. This assignment was working out well.

"So do we have to have the same terrible flying experience getting home as we did getting here?" Over the bangs and music, Sid shouted at Carmy.

Carmy shook his head, shouted back.
"No. We are going home in the Winston's
private jet."

Sid smiled and clapped his hands.
"Sweet."

CHAPTER TEN

The weather in Wisconsin did not improve in the days the group spent in Mexico. Still covered in ass-deep snow, as the plane ascended, the reality of back to real life set in.

The trip back was easier than the trip there. Mark and Paige sat together in one part of the cabin enjoying their time alone time together before the world would intrude and demand their attention.

Tom and Vivian sat together up at the front to give the couple some privacy.

"So Viv..." Tom started as he held her hand. "...think we will be in-laws?"

Vivian looked around him back to the couple. "I would say it might be possible. You okay with that?"

"More than okay. But..." His pause was enough to make her look back at him. "...what about us?"

Sitting back in her seat, she eyed him. "Us?"

"Well..." He stumbled over his words. "...do you want to get married?"

Her laughter was low, her face broke out into a smile. "Oh hell no."

"Really?" He didn't mean to have such a relieved sound in his voice.

Vivian patted his arm. "Tom dear. I love you dearly. We get along fabulously. And the sex is great." She winked at him. "But I like living alone. Having my own life. Do you really want to get married?"

Tom shook his head, looked into her eyes. "No. I like being on my own too. I don't mind Mark living with me, but from the looks of things he will moving out soon. But if you ever want to get married, just let me know. I would marry you in a heartbeat."

Leaning over to kiss him. "I will keep that offer in mind."

***

Sid and Carmy lounged on the buffet table, among the fruit, crackers and cheese. Carmy stretched out his arms. "Now this is how to travel."

Nodding, Sid agreed. This was most undeniably better than the commercial flight. "So we get them home, to work, the whole place knows they are an item. Most everyone is thrilled. Then what?"

"They get married."

Sid was unconcerned. "How hard can that be?"

"Have you ever planned a wedding and had it go off without a hitch?" Carmy chuckled.

Shrugging, Sid shook his head. "Can't say that I have."

"Oh, well here comes the fun part. Anyway he hasn't proposed properly yet. We still have some work ahead of us."

"It can't be anything like we've been through already."

"Oh, you clueless little angel, you."

***

Mark and Paige met at the coffee shop the first morning back to work. This time they were touching and laughing. Arm in arm they walked to work. Waiting for the elevator they giggled together.

Paige whispered close to Mark's

neck. "Now, once on the tenth floor we are strictly business."

His hand caressed her butt. "You mean none of that?"

Slapping his hand away. "No. None of that."

Bringing his lips to her neck, he licked her skin. "And this?"

"None of that." He was turning her on and she needed to get it stopped. Stepping away, she held him at arm's length. "This is as close as you can get. Understood?"

Mark's mischievous smiled played around his lips. "Why? Because it gets you hot and you want me?"

There was no good way to deny that, so she just looked down at her feet.

"Okay, I will be good on one condition." Mark conceded.

Paige was wary of the condition. "Oh, pray tell what is that?"

"That tonight after we get off work, we go to your place, fix dinner and I make love to you until you can't take it anymore."

Tongue in cheek, Paige met his eyes. "Think you're up to it?"

"Yes?" Mark raised one eyebrow.

"We'll see. Deal. Now act right."

The elevator doors opened. The rest of the ride up was uneventful, if Paige didn't count that she was getting excited about tonight and it was just eight o'clock in the morning.

The ding, then the sliding of the doors started Mark and Paige's journey surviving in the real world as a couple. Stepping off together, they nodded politely and separated to go to their respective offices.

Constance was waiting for Mark. He looked back at Paige for help, but she just stifled a smile to let him know he was on his own. Amy was ready to greet Paige as soon as she reached her office.

"Hey, boss. You look great. Tan, rested and..." Amy narrowed her eyes. "...laid. Oh my, you got lucky. Who? Tell me who."

Paige removed her coat and handed it to Amy. There was nothing she could get by that girl. "A lady never tells."

Entering her office, Paige was glad to be back in familiar territory.

Amy, still holding the coat, was right behind her. "So if you won't tell me who. How was it? Well that's a stupid question. I can tell by the look on your face it was good."

Stopping behind her desk, Paige snickered at Amy. "It was good. It was just what I needed. Now can we get to work? What has been happening here?" Sitting down in her chair, she glanced through her many messages.

Amy, still holding the coat, started with the office gossip. Paige listened, nodding every once in a while. Plopping back in her chair, she waited until Amy took a breath.

When her chance came. "Can you hang up my coat? And then arrange a meeting with my team?"

Amy blushed. "Sure. Sorry. On it." She turned for the door, tossing over her shoulder. "Good to have you back, and in such good spirits."

Paige chuckled to herself. "Good to be back."

***

A light snow started to fall as Mark and Paige left the office building. Walking swiftly to the small market between work and Paige's place, they talked of what to cook for dinner.

At the market, they gathered the fixings for their dinner. Salad, pasta, sauce, wine, no make that two bottles of wine. Carrying the sacks up the approach to the apartment, Mark waited as Paige unlocked the door and let them in.

Once inside, Mark sat the groceries on her breakfast bar. Paige removed her coat, hung it on a rack, kicked off her shoes. Mark took off his suit jacket as well, loosened his tie.

As Paige unloaded the goods, putting everything in a place, he surveyed the space. One big room divided into areas. Kitchen, living area, bedroom with an enclosed bathroom. In one corner there was a desk, a computer, drawing table. Pictures and papers were tacked to a bulletin board. It was the only area in disarray. Mark got the feeling that this was her creative cave.

Going around behind her, he slipped his arms around her waist. Kissing her neck, he knew dinner was going to be postponed. His fingers went to the front of her shirt. Slowly and delicately he undid a button at a time. Her body leaned back into his. Touching her skin as he moved his finger down to her breasts, stroking her nipples, he felt them rise. Removing the shirt in slow motion, his touch brushed her warm skin.

Continuing to trace under her bra straps his touch traveled down her back to the hooks. Expertly he unfastened them one at a time. The release of the garment caused her breasts to expand into his hands.

Trickling his hands over her stomach, at the waist band of her skirt, he circled around to the button at the back. Kissing her neck, he unbuttoned the skirt, lowered the zipper. The skirt fell to the floor in a gentle swish.

A low moan came from Paige as she turned to face him. As his hands caressed her butt, she lifted the loosened tie over his head. Her fingers slowly undid each of his buttons, as she kissed his chest, her fingers moved down his pleasure trail. Pulling on the belt, she locked her eyes on his as she jerked the buckle free and unsnapped his pants. Using both hands, she pushed his slacks down, slapped his butt lightly. Both of her hands moved to his front to stoke his hardened manhood. With a growl, he lifted her up and carried her to the bed. Tossing her on the soft full comforter, he gazed at the beautiful woman waiting for him to quench her sexual thirst. Climbing up her body he was on fire with his desire for her. Trying to go slow his passion was eager. But he wanted to make long sweet love to her tonight. Kissing her with all the hunger inside of him, she wrapped her arms around his neck. Trailing tiny love-bites down her neck, to the valley of her breast, he felt her hands in his hair. Taking one of her breast in his mouth, he teased and tantalized it with his tongue until he heard her moan. Moving his mouth over to the other one, she squirmed as he tormented her sensations. Traveling down to her stomach, he sucked her belly button, swirling his tongue in and around.

To her mound, his hands stroked the heated skin as she writhed under him. Parting her legs, his slow alluring tongue journeyed up her thigh, to her sweet place.

He could feel her body arch in spasms as he intensified his torturing onslaught of her arousal spot. Her fingers pulled on his hair as she twisted to meet the sweet ecstasy of his lips.

When he felt her body quiver, he rose up above her and watched as her eyes begged him to complete her gratification. As one climax crashed over her, her screams told him to enter her now. Pushing into her, her body grabbed his rod and pulled it deeper and deeper inside. His climax came with such intensity his whole body shuddered. Pumping to a rhythm, her legs wrapped around his waist allowing her to take in more of him. What started slow and easy was now strong and compelling.

Only one climax was not enough. As she reached another level, he climbed with her. Sweat from his hair dripped onto her breast. Her hair line was soaked, running down her cheeks. With her eyes closed he could see her forehead wrinkle in awareness of the passion they shared.

Their slippery bodies fused together as one last massive crashing climax rocked them together.

His chest heaved with the excitement of the afterglow of great sex. And this was great sex. When he could move again, he removed himself from her and rolled to his back next to her. Both lay panting for a few seconds. She rose up on her elbows and licked the sweat from his neck. Chuckling, he pulled her to him, kissing the top of her damp head.

"I have waited all day to do that." His voice was velvety and low.

Her body vibrating told him she was giggling. "I waited all day for you to do that."

"Paige, you know I love you."

"I do."

"So fix me dinner, woman." That brought her up from the bed.

"Excuse me?"

His teasing eyes and smile creased his face. "Dinner. I give you great sex, now you need to feed me."

With her tongue on her lips, her look was a warning. "Since I was the one that was ravished, you need to get your sweet ass up and fix me dinner."

"Ravished. I like that." He sat up, crawled off the bed. "My ravished maiden. How would you like to dine with me?" He held out his hand.

Paige scooted off the bed, took his hand. "My lord. That would be grand, but first I want a shower." Still holding his hand, she headed for the bathroom. "Care to join me?"

Allowing her to lead him. "Indeed I would."

***

As they worked together to create the meal, they talked as new lovers do exploring the likes and dislikes of each other. Together they sat at the counter in Paige's kitchenette.

Pouring Paige her second glass of wine, Mark questioned her loyalty. "You mean you are not a Packer's fan?"

She shook her head as she put a fork full of salad in her mouth. "I didn't say I wasn't a fan. I said I don't watch that much football."

Mark waved his piece of bread in the air. "You do know who the Packers are, don't you?"

"Yes, I know who they are."

His sigh was quite comical. "Well that's a relief. So what are you going to do if I want to watch a game on a Sunday afternoon?"

Taking a sip of wine. "Read a book."

"And if I want to go to a game?" Picking up his glass.

"Tell you to take your Dad and I'll go shopping."

"Well it's good to know the game rules right up front."

They clinked their glasses. Paige saw his face get serious. "What do you want to ask me?"

"Well..." He twirled the stem of the glass between his fingers. "...you know I love you. And you love me?"

Leaning back, she smiled at his insecurity. "Yes, I love you."

His eyes searched her face. "So why can't we tell anyone?"

"It would make me uncomfortable at work." Paige put her glass down.

His face showed confusion. "Why?"

"Oh, I don't know, sleeping my way to the top?" She smiled hoping he saw it as funny.

"The top of what? You're the Art Director. Do you want to be a VP? Cause I can make you a VP."

"No, I don't want to be a VP." She took his hand, squeezed it gently. "Just keep it under wraps for a while. Please?"

"Why?"

Dropping his hand, her tone took on the seriousness she so desperately wanted him to understand. "My parents went through a nasty, really nasty divorce. It involved where my father worked. I just never wanted to be put under that kind of microscope."

"Is that why you kept me at arm's length for so long?"

Paige's smile held a hint of smugness. "Yes."

His eyes narrowed with that wicked look that always melted her resolve. "So you were hot for me right from the start?"

Taking a bite of pasta, Paige tilted her head. "Don't flatter yourself."

"Tell the truth." Mark challenged.

"Okay, I was attracted to you, but I didn't want to get involved."

"So what changed your mind?"

She couldn't keep her serious tone any more. "Oh, sand, surf, many Mai Tais…"

"…And an irresistible hunk of a guy, right?" His cockiness made her laugh.

His words were hitting a mark. "That had something to do with it, I suppose." Paige took another drink of her wine.

"So someday you will decide to marry me?"

Lifting her glass to him. "Someday."

"Well darlin' the offer is always on the table."

CHAPTER ELEVEN

The night was clear, warm for the early spring. Around midnight the road was covered with a thin icy layer. Paige listened to the easy music on the car radio, not pushing her speed. Returning from a business trip to St. Paul, she was tired and glad to see the sign that said Wisconsin. Fifteen minutes at the most she would be in her parking garage, twenty-five minutes and she would be back in her comfortable bed.

***

Sid and Carmy perched on the top of the back seat. Sid was restless, fidgeting and looking out of the rear window.

Carmy had enough. "What is your problem? You're as nervous as a whore in church."

Sid did a double take. "That's an odd cliché for you to use. Unless..." He narrowed his eyes and searched the sweet, adorable angel's face.

"So I had some colorful assignments." Carmy shrugged. "Why are you so squirmy?"

Sid stood and looked straight at the front windshield. "Something is coming. Something really bad. Don't you feel it?"

Closing his eyes, wrapping his wings around him, then Carmy stood and spread them wide. "I do now."

The two angels leaped to the back of Paige's seat. Hovering, one on each side of her, they watched the road ahead. Traffic was light. There were no other cars around. Two distant headlights appeared in the oncoming lane. A three foot cement barrier separated the interstate.

"It's that car." Sid's eyes were wide as the two watched the approaching vehicle cross over the lines, side swipe the barrier and then become air born. Turning to see if Paige was reacting, they saw that she was oblivious to the pending tragedy about to happen.

Wings flapped in an irrational rhythm.

Sid bumped into the rearview mirror. Shouting at Paige. "Stop the car. Now. Go a sharp right. Get out of the way."

"She can't hear you." Carmy shouted at Sid. "You have to make her do something."

"What?" Sid saw the flying car heading straight for them.

Carmy fluttered his wings against Paige's hands on the steering wheel. She raised one and flipped it as if she was shoeing away a fly.

Stunned, Carmy started flapping around her head. Paige again swatted at the air. As she did her head turned to see a set of lights headed towards her. Grabbing the wheel tight she turned the car to the right. It spun sideways, but still in the path of the car sailing through the air. Skidding towards the stone barriers, the other car was coming down towards Paige's car.

"Carmy, do something." Sid was trying to protect Paige with his wings.

"Get her head down."

"How?"

"Sit on her."

Sid pounced on Paige's head hard enough that she let go of the steering wheel and covered her head with her arms. With one mighty push, he forced her down to the passenger seat. He spread his wings and covered her. Carmy spread his and covered her shoulders. Both angels pushed hard and held tight as the other car's wheels ripped the roof off of Paige's car shattering all the windows.

***

Mark was waiting for Paige's call that told him she was home safe. He wanted to go with her, but there was another matter just as important to deal with in Florida. They decided to split and take care of each project. Not really pleased with her decision that he take the company plane, she wanted to drive. He now wished they taken the plane together and he could have picked her up and she would be home by now.

Finishing early afternoon, he headed straight back. In the office by three, Paige texted him that she was on the road. Four hours tops she would be home.

It was seven forty-five and he still hadn't heard from her. Pacing, he caught himself letting an unknown worry overtake him. Bouncing his cell phone in his hand, he walked over to the liquor bar to pour a drink. Laying his phone on the counter, he jumped when it rang. Picking it up, his heart sank. The name Vivian was not what he wanted to see.

"Hello."

"Mark, Viv..." Her voice carried a quiver.

"What's happened?"

"Paige was in an accident..." She paused.

"Where is she?"

"Two Rivers..."

Her voice trailed off as Mark jutted out the door. Using the remote, he unlocked and started the car. Jumping in, his tire screeched as he tore out of the long circular drive. Hitting the street with a bounce, he took a sharp left and headed towards the lights of the city and Two Rivers Hospital.

Pounding the steering wheel with his fist, he didn't even want to think what the worst case scenario could be. Flying down the streets, over bridges and sliding into the parking lot, he jumped from the car and ran into the emergency entrance.

Tom met Mark at the door. His calm face greeted the panicked man. "She's okay."

Mark collapsed against his Dad. "Are you sure?"

"Yes, some scrapes and bruises, but nothing bad. She was lucky. The other car took the roof right off her car."

Mark drew back, as the horror of 'what if' stabbed him in his gut. "What happened? Can I see her?"

Wrapping his arm around Mark's shoulder, Tom guided his son down the hallway. "A car jumped the divide. Went air born. Took off her roof, landed twenty feet or so, slammed into a family in a van, flipped three times. The driver is dead. So is everyone in the van."

"And she's okay?"

"Yes." Tom lowered his voice. Pushing Mark into a dimly lit room, Vivian was sitting next to Paige's bed.

Standing at the foot of the bed, Mark looked at the beautiful woman he loved. Her neck was in a brace. A dark purple bruise swelled her cheek and eye. Several small nicks covered her face, neck and arms. Looking peaceful, she was sleeping.

Vivian came to his side. "We're blessed. She was spared. Five other people died. Two of them children."

Mark could only nod. There were no words to say how he felt. Grateful, sad, thankful, even selfish. But she was alive.

Feeling Tom and Vivian leave behind him, he moved quietly to the side of her bed. Reaching down, he took her hand. She squeezed it. That alone made the tears fall down his face. Sitting down, he raised her hand and kissed it.

"Thank you, whoever saved her." His words were like a prayer.

Four hours passed, when Mark felt a tug on his hand. He had fallen asleep from the exhaustion of worrying about Paige. With his head against the back of the chair, his gaze rested on her face. Her electric blue eyes were watching him.

"Hey." Her voice was gravelly, low.

Without moving, he smiled at her. "Hey."

When she moved her head, she jerked with pain. He came up quickly to stand at her bed. "Are you okay?"

"Yeah. It just feels like someone sat on my head." She laid it back down.

His one hand still held hers; with the other he brushed the hair from her forehead. "Well if someone did, it's a good thing otherwise you might not have it."

"It was bad, wasn't it?" Sorrow crossed her eyes.

Squeezing her hand. "Yes, it was honey. You're lucky you weren't killed."

"People died?" The horror of the realization echoed in her tone.

This was not a time to lie to her. "Yes, five."

Tears welled up in her eyes. "Oh, my God."

Wrapping his arms under her as easy as he could, her body shuddered from her sobs. He let her cry it out. When he felt her body be still, he pulled back to look at her.

"Close call. Baby."

She just nodded. "Man, this is life changing. I've been thinking..."

Stopping her with a quick kiss, he interrupted her words. "...so have I. I want to marry you. I was so afraid. Coming this close and almost losing you. That's it, I want to marry you."

"Okay." Her words were simple, she flashed a sweet smile.

Narrowing his eyes he looked at her. "Okay?"

Breaking out into a big smile, she laid her head back on her pillows. "Yes, okay. I was going to ask you. But if the macho male needs to be the one to ask, fine."

"Don't mess with me Paige. It's been a long night." The stress of the last few hours was weighing on him.

Seriousness crossed her eyes. "I'm not messing. I love you and I want to get married. So does this mean no going down on one knee? No ring?"

Relief that she had her sense of humor back, he teased her lips with his tongue, speaking against them. "You'll get your one knee. The ring. And a lifetime of love. I promise."

Taking his face in her hands she

kissed him. "Don't make promises you can't keep."

***

Carmy clasped his hands together. "Oh, how romantic. Don't you think so Sid. Sid?" The blond angel looked around the room. The dark angel was curled up in the corner of the window, shaking.

Carmy scooted over to him. "What's wrong, ole' buddy?"

Sid shook his head. "That was terrible. I hurt her."

"You saved her life. Have you never intervened with fate before?"

"No."

"No wonder you're shook up. It's hard the first time. But you need to know your instincts warned us that she was in danger. By us reacting so quickly, we kept her safe."

"But I hurt her head."

"Better it hurt than be cut off." The horror on Sid's face caused Carmy to feel so sorry for the angel. "It's okay. We did good."

Sid wiped his eyes with the back of his hand. "Is it natural for an angel to be scared?"

Carmy put his wings around Sid's

shoulder. "It's okay to be scared. We never know for sure how things will turn out. We just do the best we can. We interceded and got her through this. Now..." Carmy jumped up and did the happy dance. "...we are going to get married.

***

No one was more excited about Paige getting married than her mother. Paige could have sworn she had the florist, the caterer and wedding planner on speed dial.

True to his promise, the first night Paige was released from the hospital, Mark took her to a quiet dinner.

The restaurant was one of their favorites. On her plate was a single white rose. Champagne chilled in a bucket, candles casting a twilight glow over them.

As soon as the waiter poured the wine, Mark clinked Paige's glass.

"Knowing I love you more than life itself..." He edged from his chair and went down on one knee. "...I am asking you to marry me. To allow me to spend the rest of our lives loving you."

Paige's eyes filled with tears. Nodding she took his hand and then in the other he produced a ring box. Dark blue velvet, she knew the jeweler it came from. Using both hands, she opened the lid to be dazzled by the most gorgeous ring she ever saw. Set in white gold, the emerald cut diamond was surrounded by tiers of smaller diamonds. Mark removed it from the box and slipped it on her ring finger.

The people in the restaurant cheered and clapped as Mark rose from the floor and pulled Paige into his arms. Kissing him, she felt a release of all her fears.

"Is that a yes?" His incredible smile made her laugh.

Still unable to talk, she finally spit out the word. "Yes."

Returning to their chairs, the waiter started bringing their food.

Paige looked questionably at Mark. "When did we order?"

"We didn't. I called and arranged everything."

"And what if I said no?" She giggled at him.

"Then I would have been here for hours eating a hell of a lot of food."

Starting with their salads, the plans for the wedding began.

Mark started. "When do you want to get married?"

"Christmas Eve."

Mark looked surprised she answered so quickly. "Okay. That's eight months away. Why?"

"It was our first kiss."

He nodded in agreement. "It was. Where do you want the wedding?

"Mom's already booked the country club for the reception. St Andrew's church for the wedding."

"Really? Okay. Honeymoon?"

"Mexico." Her smile conveyed her reasons, she hoped.

"I like that. Return to the scene of the crime."

"Think you can find that cave again?"

His eyes lit up with the memory of them being stranded. "I will. Anything else I need to know?"

"Promise you will keep me sane, love me even when I am bitchy and show up on at the church on time."

"I can do that."

***

"We are getting married." Carmy was bouncing around the restaurant. Circling the chandeliers, running over the plants, jumping around the waiters.

Sid sat on the planter next to Paige. He studied her face, trying to read her emotions. On the outside she looked happy. And he believed she really loved Mark. It was taking that chance that held her back. As she stepped out of her comfort zone, he felt a protective need to shield her. While everyone gets hurt in life, he wanted love to stay true to her. To be what she only hoped but as yet did not believe in.

Carmy fluttered above Sid. "Why the gloom? She's happy. He's happy. All God's children are happy."

Sid looked up at Carmy with a snarl. "We still have some work to do. It's eight months away and a lot can happen."

"Oh, Sid lighten up, dude. Nothing is going to happen."

CHAPTER TWELVE

The night of the rehearsal dinner could not come quick enough for Paige. The planning of a wedding was the hardest thing she had ever tackled. Everybody expressed an opinion. None was the same. Nobody agreed on anything. She had tried to keep her temper away from Mark. He was always agreeable.

Just get tonight done. Be ready to walk down the aisle tomorrow at two o'clock.

Paige's mind was swirling with thoughts as she pulled into the parking lot of the country club. The night before the wedding, it was the rehearsal dinner. She had asked Mark to meet her. One last check of the room and then she would be there to welcome her guests. Smoothing down the black cocktail dress, she adjusted the strap on her Christian Louboutin heels.

"Miss Therriault." The wedding planner greeted her. Clipboard in hand, she checked off items as she explained the details to Paige. "Meet and Greet with drinks and appetizers at six o'clock. Dinner at seven thirty. Spinach salad, main entrée seared tuna with an option of pecan crushed chicken. Steamed asparagus with white cheese sauce. Rice pilaf or garlic mashed potatoes."

Paige nodded.

Entering the banquet room, she sucked in her breath. Small tea lights surrounded the windows. The tables were dressed in black tablecloths with white roses as the center piece with one red rose.

Two hands surrounded her waist. "It looks as beautiful as you." Mark's voice soothed her over-stimulated nerves.

She leaned back against him for strength.

"You okay?" His arms tightened.

"Yes." She turned in his arms. "Tell me again that by this time tomorrow night we will be in your plane on our way to Mexico?"

"Are you a member of the mile high club?" His eyes twinkled with mischief."

Paige let herself smile. "No."

"Well..." His lips tenderly kissed hers. "... tomorrow you will be."

"Kids." Tom's voice from the door interrupted them. "Looking good."

Every bit the classic gentleman, Tom Winston strolled passed the couple, hands in his pockets looking around. "Nice job, Paige. But of course, I wouldn't expect any less." He turned and winked at her. "You are my art director." Walking over to them he kissed her on the cheek.

"Where's Mom?" Paige untangled herself from Mark.

Time to do her bride thing.

"She's coming with her sister...?"

"Auntie Lane."

"Someone calling my name?" Paige turned to the sound of her Aunt Elaine's voice. Vivian walked beside her.

Paige hugged the two women. Tom offered each of them an arm and they sauntered off to the bar.

The guests started arriving in droves. Mark stood by her side, helping her with his friends. She connected hers for him.

Looking down the line, Paige saw her father and the woman he cheated with on her mother.

This is not good.

Paige searched franticly around for her Mom. Vivian and Auntie Lane were over with Tom, chatting with a group of people.

Her father edged closer. Mark leaned towards her. "What's wrong?"

"My father."

Mark followed Paige's gaze down the line of people. A tall handsome man was starring at Paige. On his arm was a younger woman, looking around like she was on the red carpet.

"The woman?" Mark whispered to Paige.

"That is 'the' woman." Paige couldn't contain the snarl in her voice.

"Oh, wow. Okay, keep your cool."

The man was now to Paige. He held out his arms. Leaning slightly in she placed her hands on his arms, keeping him a bay. "Daddy."

"My little girl. You're getting married." He turned to Mark. "William Therriault."

Mark shook his hand. "Mark Winston. Glad to meet you, sir."

The woman pushed her way between Paige and her Dad. "Pagie, dear. You look stunning."

Stiffening her body, Paige kept her arms at her side. "Sylvia. You had to come?"

"Well, yes dear. Your father and I are getting married." She flashed a huge diamond in Paige's face.

Her anger rising, she felt Mark take hold of her hand. Instead she shot a daring look at her father. "Mom's here. So is Auntie Lane. Good luck with that one."

Greeting the next guest in line, she dismissed her father and Sylvia. Out of the corner of her eyes she watched them go towards the bar. Her mother was across the room and her back to them. Now she was nervous. Her mother hated Sylvia. If the two came together there would be hell to pay. Paige told her mother that out of common courtesy she should invite him. She just thought he would have the good sense not to come.

Wrong on all accounts.

The end of the line couldn't come soon enough. As it thinned out, Paige kept turning around watching her parents. If the two met, there would be fireworks. As classy as her mother was, she could tear you a new jugular if she got a mind to.

"Paige, darling." Constance's voice was the last thing she needed.

Turn around. Smile. Be nice.

"Constance. You look great. Go have a drink."

"But can't I get one little kiss from the groom?" Her look slid down Mark's body.

"Yeah, sure kiss him." Paige darted towards her mother's group. "Mom, I have something to tell you..."

"Viv." William's voice vibrated Paige's last nerve. Watching the rage rise in her mother's eyes, Paige didn't know whether to grab her arms or duck. Looking towards Tom, she saw that he recognized her panic.

Tom put his hands on Vivian's

shoulders. Speaking over her head.
"Tom Winston."

"William Therriault."

Nodding, Tom understood now.
"The ex."

The sneer on William's face was
unmistakable. "The present?"

Mark came up behind Paige just
as Sylvia broke through the group.
That lit the fuse.

"What the fuck is she doing
here?" Vivian tried to get out of Tom's
grip. Moving her behind him, still
holding her tight. "Mr. Therriault,
maybe you and your lady friend would
like to go over by the bar."

Sylvia's voice was like nails on a
chalkboard. "The hell we will. We were
invited. It's our daughter."

Oh, shit.

Vivian was trying to claw her way
around Tom. "Your daughter. That's
it."

Paige joined Tom in holding her
mom back, while Mark tried to
reposition William and Sylvia away.

The sound of a hand slapping
skin made everyone stop as they all
turned toward the sound. Aunt Elaine

was glaring at William, as she lowered her hand. The red mark on William's face was the clue. Then Auntie Lane spoke. "You stupid, stupid man. Take you bimbo and leave. You are ruining Paige's wedding."

Holding his cheek, he spit his words. "No way old lady."

Mark grabbed Paige's Aunt as she lunged towards William. Paige felt the tears form in her eyes.

"Stop it!" Her shout made everyone in the room stop whatever they were doing and look at her.

Mark tried to reach out for her, but she shook him off. "Don't." She warned.

Sobbing she could hardly get the words out. "The wedding is off. All of you have made it a circus." Turning to her Dad. "Why did you bring her? Why did you even come?" Next her rage went to her Mother and Aunt. "Get over it. It happens to everyone. You are not unique in this aspect."

Then to Mark. "I can't get married. If it ends it just makes everyone miserable."

Kicking off her shoes she ran for

the door.

Don't go.

A voice sounded in her head, stopping her up short.

What am I doing?

She turned, looked around for Mark. There he was. With Constance in his arms, stroking his face. Her body was molded with his. Mark looked over her shoulder, saw Paige. But it was too late.

Paige continued on out to the parking lot, jumped in her car and sped away.

***

Sid and Carmy sitting on the roof, watched Paige's taillights disappear.

"Well that was a disaster."

Mark came running out, but all he saw was the fading red lights. Running his hand through his hair, he turned one way then another.

Carmy clamped his hands in front of him. "The voice was a good idea, Sid."

"It did stop her. Made her turn around, but then Constance…"

"…got in the way."

The sadness in Sid's spirit could not be

hidden from Carmy. "So close."

Carmy slapped him on the back. "Hey, we're not done yet. Let's regroup and go for another route to the plan. It's not over till the fat woman sings."

"What fat woman? Are you talking about Auntie Lane? I wouldn't call her fat. That's just rude."

Carmy chuckled. "It's a saying."

***

Slamming the door to her loft, Paige ripped the dress off. Stepping over it, her cell phone rang. Looking at the caller ID she turned the phone off. Going to her fridge, she jerked out a half opened bottle of wine. Removing the cork with her teeth, spitting it in the sink. Not even bothering with a glass, she chugged the liquid down like it was orange juice. Her land line phone started to ring. She yanked it out of the wall and threw it across the room.

Giant sobs raked her body. Falling down on the bed she cried until sleep finally quieted the pain. At some point during the night she heard a knock on her door.

"Go away! Please."

The knocking stopped and she heard footsteps fade away.

The sun coming through her east window woke her up. Feeling like she had been drugged, she staggered to the bathroom. Splashing cold water on her face, she raised her head to look in the mirror.

God, you look pathetic.

Her mouth dry, she shuffled to the kitchen. On the way she saw a white envelope on the floor that someone had slid under the door. Opening it, she found one airline ticket for Mexico. It left in two hours. A note was with it:

Go away for awhile.
Think things over.
Love, Mom

Paige thought while she tapped the ticket on her hand.

Why the hell not.

Her bags were packed. A quick shower and she could be gone. Away from the madness she called her life.

***

As soon as she got to the hotel, everything was arranged for her. The bell boy took her bags and showed her to a suite. It was different than the one she had before, so no bad memories. Looking out the sliding doors, the ocean called to her to dip her feet into the surf.

The warm beach was cushiony under her bare feet. When she reached the tide line, she dug her toes into the wet sand. Standing still as the waves ebbed back and forth, gave a feeling of moving. Taking the first deep calming breath she had been allowed for several months started to clear her head.

What have I done? I so screwed this up.

"I think you left these behind." Mark's voice echoed behind her.

Turning around she saw him standing back from her with her black and red Christian Louboutins dangling from his fingertips.

"I kind of feel like Prince Charming looking for Cinderella."

Tears filled her eyes.

"Oh, please don't cry." He

eliminated the distance between them. Gathering her in his arms he rocked her back and forth.

Speaking in muffled tones against his shirt. "How did you get here?"

"I came in my plane." He pulled back to look at her. "You know, my plane?"

Crying and laughing at the same time. "I am so sorry…"

"Shhh…" His lips stopped her words. Speaking against her mouth. "What can I do to get you to marry me? I'll beat up your father. And Sylvia. I'll quit the agency. I'll…"

"You would do that for me?"

"What? Beat up your father? Or Sylvia?"

Chuckling. She loved him so. "Quit the agency?"

His face turned serious. "If that's what it took, I would."

"That is so sweet." Her resolve was melting.

"So is that what you want?"

"What I want is to marry you, right here. On the beach at sunset."

He winked at her. "You got it

baby." ***

The two angels stood and watched the lovers share a passionate kiss.

Sid, the dark doubting angel had to ask. "So is this going to happen this time?"

Carmy the sweet optimistic angel threw his arm around Sid's shoulder. "It will."

"So what do we do now?" Sid looked over at Carmy.

Turning around, Carmy walked with Sid down the beach. "Sid, I think this is the start of a beautiful friendship."

Made in the USA
Coppell, TX
24 August 2022

81973100R00125